ESCAPE FROM PARADISE
By Kay Wahlgren

ESCAPE FROM PARADISE

First edition. August 25, 2024.

ISBN: 979-8230781226

Written by Kay Wahlgren.

Also by Kay Wahlgren

Elbow Chronicles
Ladies' Man
Escape From Paradise

Table of Contents

CHAPTER 1: ANGIE

When you wake up with a cat on your head, you know it's going to be a bad day. Elbow rolled over and reached for the squirt gun. The cat, Bunky by name, did not take kindly to the maneuver and dug his claws into Elbow's scalp.

"Yeow!" Elbow jumped up, swinging wildly, squirting water in every direction. "Damn cat!" The cat suddenly had second thoughts about remaining on Elbow's head and made a mad leap for the thin slit of open window above the bed. He squeaked through just before Elbow slammed down the sash.

"That's right, you mangy, six-toed wonder! You run! Don't even think about getting back in here!"

Angie sat up in bed and ran her fingers through her spiky, neon pink hair. "What was that?"

"It was that fiend, Bunky. He got me good."

Elbow bumped his head on the single lightbulb dangling from a cord above his head in the six by nine foot garden shed. He turned it on and looked in the mirror on the wall across from the bed. Blood trickled down onto his ear. "Damn. Look what that stupid cat did to me. You feed 'em, be nice to 'em, and look how they treat you."

He stepped off the makeshift bed and walked two steps to get a closer look in the mirror. He reached for the toilet paper roll and tore off small squares to apply to his wounds to stop the bleeding.

Angie squinted at him. "Yeah, nice look with all the toilet paper. You used that damn squirt gun again, didn't you? You're a rotten shot. My hair is all wet. I'll bet you didn't get the cat wet at all."

"He didn't stand still long enough for me to get a good hit. Besides, I was aiming in the dark."

"You even got the wall." She frowned.

"Just go back to sleep."

"I can't. The bed's all wet too."

"Well, sleep on this side. It's drier."

"God, this place is a dump. We're sleepin' in a plastic garden shed! The bed takes up almost the entire space."

"The mattress gets tipped up against the wall during the day so we can walk around," he explained.

"Yeah, 'walk around'. You can stand in one spot to brush your teeth in the bucket and make coffee on the 'kitchen' shelf at the same time."

"Hey, it's better than getting hassled by the cops for sleeping under someone's hedge on the street. At least it's out of the rain."

"Ha! It leaks like a sieve. And I'm gettin' tired of having an audience of green lizards every time I take a shower under the garden hose outside."

"The rent's free! Nobody cares about this abandoned shed. With all the tall weeds, you can't see it behind the garage. Nobody even looks. It's private."

"Yeah, private—you could die here and nobody would find you until after the next hurricane!" She got up. "Move over. I gotta dry off."

Elbow moved over, sat down on the mattress, and looked at her as she dried off the tattoos on her arms. She was right. It was cramped, but it provided the basic necessities. So what if the roof needed a blue tarp to keep the rain out, or the water supply came from a secret connection to a neighbor's hose under the shrubbery, or the hot plate and light bulb were on a hidden extension cord plugged into the other neighbor's garage. He had lived in worse places.

Maybe what made it cramped was Angie. She didn't seem to appreciate the finer points of their relationship. Lately it was nothing but whine, whine, whine—the roof, the shed, the shower, even the bed. Nothing was right. She wasn't happy. Maybe it was time they parted company.

"Look, Angie, if this place bugs you so much, you could just pack up and find someplace else."

There. It had been brewing for weeks. He'd finally said it.

"What? You tryin' to kick me out? Is that what you want?"

"Not exactly, but you complain about it all the time. Maybe you got something else in mind."

"You no good son-of-a...! You want to kick me out into the cold?"

"Cold? This is Key West. Even in winter it's seventy-five degrees!"

She started throwing things. First the coffee pot, then the bucket whizzed past his head and caught him in the shoulder. There aren't a lot places to hide in a six by nine foot garden shed. He took refuge in the corner near the door. She stood on the bed and continued the barrage with anything she could get her hands on.

Elbow saw his chance. He lifted up the side of the bed. Angie fell onto the mattress and he tilted the whole thing up flat against the wall with her sandwiched in between. She screamed bloody murder and kicked against the side of the shed, rocking the whole thing from side to side.

This was not going well. Luckily he kept all his clothes in a plastic bag out of habit. He had better grab it and his shoes and run before she figured out how to move the mattress and get out from under it. He slipped into his jeans and struggled to get his feet into a pair of sneakers. He grabbed the plastic clothing bag and escaped out the door into the alley.

There was a loud popping sound. The shower hose coupling attached to the roof suddenly gave way. Water shot out in a great cascade, draining through holes in the roof. A sudden flash of blue light came from inside the shed and a bigger pop sounded from inside the neighbor's garage. Water hit the extension cord and shorted out everything back to the garage and maybe beyond. *Oh hell!*

Angie screamed. Elbow was tempted to run, but the gentleman in him couldn't leave her trapped in the shed so he ran back. When he opened the door he smelled smoke. Damn! Angie was on the floor trying to untangle herself from the bedsheets. She was in a fighting mood and took a swing at him. He picked her up and threw her over his shoulder trailing bedsheets behind him. He deposited her in the alley. She took another swing and this time connected with his chin.

"What did you do that for?" He held his jaw.

"You honking idiot! You trapped me in that mattress! What were you trying to do, kill me?" She aimed another roundhouse at his head.

He grabbed her hand and spun her around to face the shed. "Whoa, I think I just saved your life. Look."

The inside of the shed was in flames. Little green lizards were beating a hasty escape up the sides of the garage to safety. Smoke was curling up into the air.

All the fight had gone out of her. She stood there with her mouth open. "It's on fire," she said meekly.

Elbow picked up one of the sheets and wrapped it around her bare shoulders. "Go knock on one of the neighbor's doors and tell them to call the fire department."

"What?"

"Fire department! Go!" He yelled. She ran across the alley. He approached the shed and managed to grab the garden hose off the roof. It was still spitting water in all directions. He aimed most of the spray inside the door at the mattress and sides of the interior, but the heat from the burning plastic was pretty intense, and he had to back off. Angie returned to the alley. The fire department was on its way.

"My clothes!" she wailed. "All my stuff is in there!"

The sirens grew closer. Elbow was allergic to sirens. They always meant cops. He rummaged in his wallet. "Here, this is all I got left from my last payday. Buy yourself some new stuff, Angie, I got to disappear. You should do the same. People will ask questions. They are going to want to pin this on someone, especially if that garage goes up in flames."

She looked at him and the fire and nodded. He shouldered his plastic bag and did a fast trot down the alley, stopping near the bush at the corner for a quick look as the fire trucks arrived. Angie was gone. Time for him to disappear too.

CHAPTER 2: THE SHARK'S NEST

E lbow hotfooted it for several blocks, putting some distance between himself and the fire. Everything was going to be pretty charred by the time they put it out. There wouldn't be much left to connect either him or Angie to the shed. It was an accident, but the cops may not believe that. Maybe it was time to leave Key West until things cooled down.

He'd met Angie one night on the beach. She was fond of tequila and he had put back his share of beer. They hit it off right away with her spiky, neon hair and giggly laugh. She moved in without much ceremony and suddenly they were an item, but she never seemed to enjoy *la vida loca* the way he did. This was Key West. Here the weather was mostly sunny. The real residents, the conchs, were a simpatico bunch and the living was easy.

He even had a job. It was a crap job with crap pay cleaning up the Shark's Nest bar near the pier after hours, but it brought in a few bucks, at least enough to buy beer and a new pair of jeans every now and then. What more did a guy need? The rest of the day was free to sip a few on the beach and sleep.

Angie complained about it, but he thought the shed was perfect. Camouflaged nicely with overgrown shrubs behind a garage, no one knew it was there. They'd fixed it up pretty good with a light bulb and a hot plate and a bed that was a real mattress. He had plans to put a screen on the window and set up inside running water. All he had to figure out was how to make a decent drain.

All that was gone now, including Angie. If she was smart she would bunk with her cousin for a while and then take a long vacation out of town. His own plans were a little sketchy. He needed sleep and a chance to sort things out.

He checked the lump in the bottom of his shoe. It was his emergency stash. Last time he counted it there were twenty-three secret dollars hiding there, enough for emergency beer but not for a bus ticket back to Miami.

He headed for the Shark's Nest. The back window was sometimes open. Maybe he could get in there. He could sleep on the pool table for a few hours, and if Tootsie, the owner, found him he could say he was there all night. Yeah, good plan.

A faint, orange light showed in the eastern sky. He stopped at the corner and looked around. There was usually a squad car parked somewhere along the row of bars and shops near the pier. It was gone. The cop was probably called away to the fire. Well, at least the fire was good for something.

He ventured out into the street, crossed it and slid into the narrow walkway between the Shark's Nest and the Mystical Crystal next door. The window was near the back, above the garbage cans. It was open just an inch or two. Elbow climbed onto one of the cans and pulled the window open wide enough to crawl through. It made a creaking sound. He froze and looked around.

When he was sure he coast was clear, he put the plastic bag inside, launched himself head-first inside and struggled to get his legs and feet through the small opening while his body dangled over the end of the bar in the pool room. He managed to get both legs through, then dropped like a rock onto the plastic bag and slid off onto the floor.

"Well, that was graceful," he said.

He squinted around the interior trying to see in the dark. He could make out the shapes of pool tables lined up across the room. He picked the far one, stashed his bag underneath and laid down on the green surface. Man, it was hard. Pool tables always look so cushy but they really aren't. He tried rolling over. A guy would have to be really tired or drunk to sleep on a pool table. He stood up and walked toward the sliding glass doors to the porch that stretched out over the water. There were a couple of deck chairs outside chained to the railing that might do.

He stared in a mirror on the wall advertising one of Milwaukee's finest and picked tiny squares of toilet paper out of his sandy colored hair. He took a hard look at the bruise beginning to form on his chin where Angie clipped him. Maybe a couple day's growth of beard might cover it. The ladies always thought that was cool. All in all he was a fairly good looking dude, not muscle bound like some of those college, beach bodies perhaps, but trim and fit in a rough sort of way. At least he still had all his teeth. He tried his winning, boyish grin in the mirror. The mirror smiled back its approval.

He heard the window creaking above the bar and flattened himself in the dark against the wall and watched the window. Someone was trying to get in.

He hadn't been very quiet or careful with his entry acrobatics. Did someone hear him? The owner or the police would use the door. This had to be a genuine intruder.

While the guy tried to angle himself through the window, Elbow crouched in the aisle between the pool tables where he could watch the window and slide out of sight under the pool table if necessary.

This guy had a different approach. He came feet-first through the window. How the hell did he do that, Elbow wondered. Then the guy touched a toe to the bar without looking and pulled his body and torso inside. It looked like he had done it before. Even though he was breaking in, you had to admire the guy's agility.

A small flashlight switched on and panned around the room. Elbow ducked out of sight. When the flashlight beam passed, he rose again and watched as the light concentrated on the bar area. On a box near the door, a small red light blinked on and off. He hadn't noticed that before. A silent alarm? If so, this could get interesting. It could be a real party if the cops joined in.

The flashlight beam held steady near the end of the bar. The idiot was trying to get into the cash register. Tootsie, the owner, always emptied it every night and took the proceeds home with her in her ample cleavage. Everybody knew you didn't mess with Tootsie. She was close to three hundred pounds of burley attitude. She once put a headlock on some poor fellow who was partying too hard and almost tore off his ear. The locals knew how to behave themselves at Tootsie's. This guy must be uncommonly dumb or a tourist.

Elbow watched the glare of headlights pass by outside. Maybe Iggy, the night cop, was done with the fire and was checking out the place. Iggy was tight-assed about the law and very quick with the handcuffs. Key West was laid back about most things, but Iggy was strictly by the book, so they gave him the late night shift when most people were in bed and not committing the sin of leaving their shoes on the beach or acting silly on the sidewalk.

From the clicks and rattles Elbow could tell the guy at the bar was not having any luck with the cash register. His flashlight beam suddenly ran along the rows of bottles on the shelf against the wall. The guy picked out an expensive bottle or two of scotch and the best vodka and slipped them in a sort of carry sack he wore across his chest. He was certainly a pro and didn't want to leave empty-handed.

CHAPTER 3: COPS AND ROBBERS

The front door lock clicked. Uh-oh—the shit was about to hit the fan. Two sets of flashlight beams crisscrossed the floor and walls in the front room.

"If this is some sort of wild goose chase, Iggy, I'll wring your scrawny neck," Tootsie's voice thundered. "It's four a.m. I need my beauty sleep."

"Quiet! Iggy said. "I told you, the alarm went off. There's someone in here."

The intruder froze and made a move to the top of the bar near the open window and started to fit himself through the opening. Elbow argued with himself. Should he do it? What the hell, it was now or never! He stood up and sprinted to the bar and grabbed one of the guy's legs just as he was slipping his body through the opening. The guy yelled and kicked out with his free leg.

"Stop! Police!" Iggy yelled and assumed a full SWAT team stance, gun drawn and aimed at Elbow's head.

Tootsie flipped on the lights. "Don't be a fool, Iggy. That's Elbow. Can't you see he's got the bugger?" She waddled to the bar and grabbed the guy's other leg. He was in for it now. She twisted it. The guy screamed. She pulled him back through the window and across the bar almost dragging Elbow with him. The bottles in the carry sack clinked as she flipped the intruder to the floor with a quick wrestling move.

"You gonna stand there playing NCIS, Iggy, or you gonna help me corral this idiot?" she snarled.

Iggy kept the gun aimed at the general commotion and did a good imitation of Miami PD with a knee on the guy's back and shiny handcuffs on his wrists. It was overkill. Tootsie had a death grip on the guy's leg. He wasn't going anywhere.

She finally let go and hoisted him onto a bar stool by his neck. "Okay, mister, let's see what you got in that bag."

"I'll search him, Tootsie, you just stand back," Iggy told her.

She ignored Iggy and reached in for the bottles. "Ha! My best scotch! At least the sucker's got good taste."

Iggy reached for his gun again. He aimed it at Elbow. "You, up against the wall! What are you doing here at four in the morning?"

"For crumbs sake, Iggy, you gun crazy or something? Elbow is the night guy. He cleans up the beer bottles and broken glass. You got eyes. He was hangin' onto the guy's foot tryin' to keep him from leaving."

"What if they're in cahoots? This Elbow guy lets him in and they split the take?"

"Through the window? You got bullets for brains, Iggy. Then they both woulda used the door, not the window. Besides the only thing worth stealin' in here is the booze. The till's empty at night. Put that gun away before you shoot somebody and mess up the bar."

Iggy wasn't convinced and held Elbow against the wall. He kicked his legs into a spread position. Iggy's cop-mode was turned on full blast. Elbow was beginning to sweat.

"Don't make me come over there and take that fool gun away from you!"

Iggy backed off and holstered the gun, but kept his hand on it just in case. Elbow breathed a little easier.

"Here, Iggy. Take hold of this guy and read him his rights and get him outa here."

The guy hissed at her. "Take your hands off of me, Fatso."

Tootsie grabbed the guy's neck and held up his head. "Well aren't you a sweetheart." She released his throat and let him breathe. He had a spiked mohawk and a nasty scar on the bridge of his nose. Tootsie gave him a hard look. "I don't recognize him. He's not a regular. Lock him up and take his prints."

"You don't have to tell me how to do my job," Iggy told her.

"Yeah, right. See you later, officer." She gave him a Cub Scout salute.

The guy didn't go quietly. He growled. "Hey you, broken glass boy, I got your number. I'm comin' for you!" Iggy grabbed the intruder's arm and made him bend over as he duck-walked him out the door.

Tootsie turned her gaze on Elbow and laughed. "Iggy was wound up a little tight tonight with the fire and all. Okay, hotshot, the dork policeman is gone. Tell me what the hell you were doing here at four a.m."

Elbow put on his wide-eyed, innocent look. "I got tossed out of the place where I live and I didn't have any place to go. I was cleanin' up last night and I was awful tired so I just curled up on the pool table. Then I heard the window creak and there was this guy climbing in so I hunkered down to see what he was doing 'cause he might have a gun or something and he was messing around near the cash register and then he started picking out bottles on the shelf and putting them in his sack and fixin' to climb out the window so when I heard you coming in the front door I ran and grabbed his leg and held on." He paused to take in some air. Most of it was sort of true. He just left out a few details.

Tootsie squinted, trying to digest the story. "...Okay. I'll buy it. But you find someplace else to crash from now on and make sure that window is closed when you clean up. I got to pull down the storm shutters. Big storm coming."

"A big storm? But there's not a cloud in sight."

"You haven't lived here long have you, honey?"

"Do you mind if I sleep on one of the deck chairs on the porch? Just until it gets light? I'm mighty tired."

"Sure. But don't sleep too long. You get yourself off someplace safe." She waddled over to the glass door to the deck and opened it. Elbow grabbed his plastic bag of clothes and exited outside. Tootsie pulled down the security gate, locked the door and the window, turned off the lights, and left.

Well that turned out better than Elbow expected. He could have been in jail right now or mincemeat on the floor if Tootsie hadn't liked his story. The woman was not known for small talk or genteel manners. Her size alone was enough to make most people back off. Couple that with her blunt personality and the skull and crossbones tattoos and she was a real charmer.

This was turning out to be quite a day, rescuing a lady in distress from a fire and helping catch a robber. He wasn't used to being such an upright citizen. If he wasn't careful someone might pin a medal on him and spoil his reputation.

CHAPTER 4: STORM WARNING

All the lounge chairs and tables on the deck were chained to the railing to discourage them walking away at night. Elbow picked out the one on the end, wrestled it free enough to let it stand up and made himself comfy. He checked to see if the pelicans had left any deposits before he sat down. They were always there on the deck, looking for fishermen to throw them a morsel. Strange, the pelicans were all gone. He looked at the sky again. It was brilliant orange as the sun made its way above the line of clouds on the horizon to the east. What storm?

He looked across the water to the pier. It was busy with people and their boats. Some of the boats were deluxe. Boat life looked pretty nice. You could fish for your supper, lay back with a drink, watch the sunset, and move around anywhere. Sweet.

"Hey you—you up on the deck chair! Help me out here."

Elbow looked around. A tall sailboat mast was up against the porch railing. The boat was just over the side of the deck. An older guy with a gray beard was holding onto a piling underneath.

"Take this rope and tie it up for me will you?"

The rope landed on the porch floor at Elbow's feet. He did as the guy asked and tied it around one of the porch railings. He leaned over the edge to get a good look at the boat. It was not exactly a deluxe model, but the lady at the back was. She had red hair and was dressed in short shorts and a blue tank top. Elbow admired the way she filled it out.

The boat was a twenty-foot fiberglass sailboat, patched in several places. There was a small cabin in the middle and a rather large motor clamped to the back. A small electric motor was attached to the side. It was so quiet he'd never heard the boat glide in.

"Thanks. You think I could tie it up here for a while? The rest of the pier is full right now," the gray-haired fellow said.

"The owner might object, but I don't," Elbow said with a smile at the redhead. "Need help with anything else?"

"We're just loading on some supplies. It won't take long," the guy said and motioned for the red head to move up on the porch.

"Where are you headed?" Elbow asked her.

"Up the coast a bit. Could you watch the boat for us? I just need a few things. Be back in a flash."

"Sure. No problem."

"Move it, Marcie," the guy grunted. "We're in a hurry." He handed her a box, then busied himself with the motor on the back. The redhead extended her hand, and Elbow helped her up on the porch deck.

"Thanks, hon." She walked around the side of the Shark's Nest to the street.

Elbow watched her walk away and smiled. Oh my, she was fine. Maybe he could parlay his helpfulness into some long distance transportation. Who knows, if Mr. Gray Hair wasn't her boyfriend, it might be the beginning of a beautiful friendship and a ride out of Dodge. He wasn't too anxious to meet the Shark's Nest intruder again.

He settled back in the deck chair. He usually didn't get up this early. He watched as boats geared up and left the harbor. It certainly was busy this early in the morning. The only thing missing was the army of gulls and pelicans, especially that big pelican with the orange leg tag that bothered customers during the day. All the birds were gone. Maybe it was too early for them. Anyway, the air was warm, the wind was calm and the sea was as smooth as a sheet of glass, just like a picture postcard.

The redhead returned with several plastic grocery bags.

"Here, let me help you with those," Elbow offered. "You get on board and I'll hand them down to you."

"Thanks, hon," she said.

He helped her down onto the boat and handed her the bags one by one.

"Say, you wouldn't need another hand on the boat would you? I'm looking to leave Key West and I don't have wheels right now."

"Where are you headed?"

"Anywhere, I guess. It's sort of the off season here, and work is a little scarce." He smiled.

She looked at him and smiled in return. "Okay. I'll ask my pa. You don't want to be here during the hurricane anyway."

"Hurricane? It's a beautiful day."

"Don't you watch the news? That bank of clouds on the horizon is a tropical storm that promises to be a hurricane by mid-afternoon." She disappeared into the cabin. Elbow could hear loud words being exchanged but couldn't tell what they were saying.

When she returned, she smiled. "Hop on. We can give you a ride as far as Flamingo. The Keys and the islands there give a lot of protection if the center of the storm doesn't ride over the top."

"Thanks, that sounds great." He grabbed his bag of clothes and climbed over the porch railing onto the boat deck. Where the hell was Flamingo? Was that a town? He had never heard of it. Wherever it was, it wasn't Key West.

CHAPTER 5: MARCIE

The redhead's 'pa' emerged from the cabin and looked Elbow up and down without much enthusiasm. "You been on a boat before?"

"Afraid not. I'm pretty good with motors, but not with port and starboard. I learn pretty fast. Just tell me what to do."

Gray Hair gave Marcie a look, but she just ignored it. "Start by untying that line on the pier and stow it here so no one gets tangled in it."

"Aye, aye, Captain—or don't they say that anymore?"

"This isn't Pirates of the Caribbean, Peg Leg, just a sailboat."

Elbow almost said "Aye, aye" again but thought better of it and tried to do an efficient job of untying the granny knot he'd used on the porch railing.

"What's your name?" The man asked.

"Elbow."

"Elbow, huh?" His eyes looked up at the sky. Elbow looked up too. The sun was still above the clouds but not by much.

"You worried about the storm?" Elbow asked

"Always. Can you swim?"

"Why do you ask?"

"This could get a little rough."

"Maybe you shouldn't go," Elbow advised.

"What? Are you nuts? The boat would end up a pile of fiberglass on the main street with the storm surge. Why do you think everyone's leaving? If we can make it to the islands or the coast, we stand a better chance. Besides, I got business up the coast. If you're coming with us, stow your gear in the cabin so it won't come loose and roll around. We can't stay here all day."

Elbow climbed on board and went below. It was a cramped cabin with two small bunks angled toward one another in the bow with cabinets below. He stuffed his plastic bag in one of the cabinets and returned to the deck.

The shapely redhead held out her hand and gave him a smile. "By the way, I'm Marcie. My dad is Ed." She nodded toward Gray Hair. "You don't get seasick, do you?"

"Ah no, I don't think so."

She handed him a life vest. "Put this on, hon. Sit here and don't touch anything unless we tell you to, okay?"

Elbow did as he was told. Marcie used the electric motor to guide the sailboat skillfully past the other boats on the pier out to open water. She gave the clouds a glance and turned the boat north. There was a slight breeze from the south.

Once on open water, Ed switched to the large motor on the back. Elbow watched as Key West grew smaller and smaller behind them and soon disappeared from view.

Elbow gripped the side rail as the boat plowed through the water. The patches on the fiberglass hull were more visible now. Maybe this wasn't the best decision he ever made. He tried to keep his mind off images of *The Perfect Storm*. Marcie came and sat next to him. He cleared his throat and tried to act casual. "How long have you been sailing?" he asked.

"About ten years. I used to race, but it got to be ultra-competitive. For some guys, everything from drinking to dating is a competition. I like a simpler life. Just the basics, no hassles."

Elbow noticed the water wasn't smooth any more. Small swells were pushing the boat forward, gently lifting it up and down as they moved on.

"We can put up the sail now and save the motor for later," Ed announced. "Here, Elbow, you take the motor. Keep us in a straight line with the compass while we raise the sail."

Elbow managed a nervous smile and took his place at the motor. He watched Marcie untie the canvas, and hoist it to the top of the mast.

It slowly filled with air as she adjusted the boom to gain the most speed from the wind angle.

She took her place at the tiller and turned off the motor. "The sky is clouding over. The wind should increase and give us a good ride. Sit on the deck if you don't want to get whacked by the boom if it swings around."

The boat leaned to one side. Elbow backed up to wedge himself in the corner between the side and rear seats. Ed laughed.

"Don't panic yet, hon," Marcie told him. "I'll tell you when. It may get a little rough if the wind increases, and then we will really lean over. It just means we are going faster and will get there sooner."

"That's almost comforting. I'm not exactly a boat man. The closest I get to large bodies of water is a bathtub."

"So, why are you called Elbow? Or is that your real name?" She asked.

"A childhood altercation with my brother. My elbow knocked out a few of his teeth. It was an accident, but all I had to do was raise my elbow at him and he'd stopped hassling me. I became known in the neighborhood as *The Elbow*."

"What's your real name?"

"I forgot."

She laughed. "Where are you from?"

"Miami mostly. You said you were headed to Flamingo. Is that a town or a bar or what?"

"It's a small place on the south coast, mostly surrounded by the Everglades. The hurricane did a number on it the last time. There's a place to hide out on an island offshore if it gets really bad."

"Marcie!" Her dad snapped. "Quit gabbing and watch the wind."

She looked at the sky and waves again and adjusted the sail. The wind was picking up. The sail was beginning to really pull at the lines.

"Is Flamingo where you live?" Elbow asked.

She gave her dad a glance. "We...ah, move around a bit."

CHAPTER 6: STORM SURGE

They sailed on for hours. Marcie kept one hand on the tiller and the other on the line to the end of the boom, adjusting it to catch the most wind. Whatever she was doing looked complicated. She seemed to do it automatically with the swells and gusts of wind to keep the boat on a steady course.

Ed turned on the radio for storm updates. The noon news wasn't encouraging. In a matter of hours, the storm had become a Category 2 monster feeding on the warm energy of the Gulf Stream. It was poised to make a hit on the Bahamas and head northward along the Miami coast or else swing farther out to sea.

The boat soared up and plunged down the merciless five and six foot waves. Elbow's stomach was empty but it still wanted to climb up into his throat and launch over the side. He turned a lovely shade of green. This was definitely not the best decision he had ever made.

Thrashes of rain beat down on them as the boat navigated waves that crashed over the bow. Marcie broke out rain ponchos, but everyone was already soaked.

"Here, Elbow, grab this boom line and hold tight until I tell you to let up just a little. I need both hands on the tiller."

Elbow was glad to have something else to concentrate on besides his queasy stomach.

"Keep her steady!" Ed shouted.

"Trying to but the wind is shifting," Marcie shouted back. "Don't know how much longer the sail will reach the wind before we have to use the motor. It's full out right now!"

"It's getting darker. We're still on course according to GPS. If you're tired, give it to me and I'll hold it as long as I can!" Ed told her.

The boom suddenly swung around. Elbow dropped and kissed the deck. The sail flapped wildly.

"Hold this!" Marcie shouted handing off the tiller to him.

She jumped into action. She and Ed scrambled to control the canvas before the wind tore it to shreds and the boom with it. Elbow stayed low on the deck holding onto the tiller with all his might, trying to keep the boat on compass point.

They managed to lower the canvas, tie it to the boom and secure it to the cradle above the motor in the rear. Without the force of the wind on the sail to work against the tiller in the water, the boat was adrift, at the mercy of the wind and sea. The boat turned sideways in the trough of waves and lurched back and forth as cresting swells threatened to wash over the sides.

Ed flipped a switch on the large motor and pulled the starter cord. Nothing. Elbow abandoned the useless tiller and sprang up to cover the top of the motor with his rain poncho as a wave cascaded over onto the deck. Ed pulled again. This time there was a sputter of life. He pulled again and the motor roared, sending all of them sprawling backward. Ed quickly grabbed the handle to gain control and set the boat in a better direction against the waves. "That was close," he said. "Go help Marcie put up the cockpit cover so we can keep most of the water out of here."

Marcie was already struggling with the plastic tarp, trying to loop it over the boom so it could be fastened to the railings on both sides of the boat and make a sort of tent over the cockpit. Elbow stood up on the swaying, lurching deck. Water sloshed around his ankles. It was slippery. He hugged the boom and hung on for dear life. He made his way with tiny sideways steps to the mast as the boat did roller coaster moves on the waves.

"Nice job, Elbow. Guess we needed an extra hand after all." She gave him a smile.

Her yellow rain poncho kept getting in the way, so she took it off. Her water-soaked tee shirt clung to her body. Oh my, she was fine! Elbow had a hard time concentrating on tying the flapping ends of the tarp to the railing.

"Marcie, you get below," Ed ordered. "Two people will take two hour shifts manning the motor. I know it's rough, but try to get some rest. In spite of everything, we've been pretty good keeping on course. I'm heading for the islands instead of the coast. They're closer. If we're lucky we'll hit Hog Hill Island head on."

Hit Hog Hill Island head on. Elbow wished Ed had used some other terminology. Rain was pelted down on the plastic tarp in the growing dark. Visibility was down to zero except when lightning lit the sky. Now there was something else to worry about besides giant waves, patched fiberglass, swinging booms, and lightning.

Elbow's eyes followed Marcie as she climbed down into the cabin. From any angle, she was a treat to look at. She paused at the top of the stairs and gave him a wink, then smiled, before she disappeared below.

"Your job is to be a safety backup in case I fall asleep or go overboard. Keep your eyes on the compass and off of Marcie. You got that, Elbow?"

The boat rode the monotonous waves up, down, and sideways. Even though Ed told him not to think about Marcie, Elbow's mind wandered. Some women just give off special vibes. He knew it from the moment he saw her under the pier at the Shark's Nest. And when she walked away from him down the porch in Key West, he knew she knew his eyes would follow her.

The two-hour shift passed slowly. The endless waves seemed to be coming from a different direction, or maybe the waves were the same and the boat had turned. They were pushing the boat from behind instead of beating it on the side.

Marcie appeared at the top of the hatch to take her watch. Ed handed over the motor to Elbow and grunted a few instructions. "Keep the heading just like this. Marcie, you hold the compass and the GPS and head toward that first island just on the edge of the map. That's probably Hog Hill." He looked at the sky between lightning flashes.

"Call me if anything changes." He gave them both a wary eye and disappeared into the cabin and closed the hatch.

Marcie sat down beside Elbow and looked at the compass. She put her hand over his on the tiller and turned the motor slightly. She kept her hand there. "You've never sailed before, have you?" she asked.

"Never."

"How do you like it?"

"I'd like it a lot better without the hurricane."

She laughed, a throaty laugh, not a little girl's giggle. She let go of his hand and undid a latch on one of the side seats. She opened it, reached inside and brought out two beers. "Here, hon, you've earned this."

He was grateful for the offer, but for the first time in his life, the thought of beer made him sick.

Two hours later Ed reappeared and Marcie took over the motor.

"We're getting close," she said.

Ed looked at the GPS. "Tighter to the northeast should do it. I'll bet you my best socks that's Hog Hill Island on the map."

"That's a strange name, Hog Hill," Elbow said.

"All those little island dots have weird names," Marcie said, "but that one really does have a hill. Sort of, anyway. It's part of Everglades National Park. No one really lives there, but we kind of camp out there sometimes."

Ed cleared his throat and shot her a glance. "What's the compass say there, Elbow, we still on course?"

"Spot on," he answered. For some reason Ed was a bit touchy about Hog Hill Island. Elbow let the subject drop and pretended to be engrossed keeping the boat on a steady course. He wasn't keen to walk the plank or get tossed overboard for being overly curious.

Another course correction to east-northeast made the boat shudder as it climbed up and plunged down at an angle over the top of six-foot waves. Ed and Marcie didn't seem too worried, but Elbow prayed the boat could take all the twisting and thudding drops without creating new cracks and holes in the already patchwork hull.

Ed suddenly stood and pointed. "There! Off to the right. A light. See it? There it goes again. It could be the buoy off Sand Point. Aim for it—a little more to starboard."

Elbow held onto the railing and stood up. He squinted against the rain pelting him in the darkness. A faint light seemed to blink on and then off when they crested the waves. Whatever it was, it was a welcome sight. It meant civilization and perhaps even safety from the constant battering of the storm. The light grew brighter as they closed in on it. They could hear the bell as the buoy rocked wildly in the waves.

Ed gave directions. "Marcie, bring us as close as you can. To the right so we don't bottom out on the sand. I'll get a light on it. If I can read the number on the side, I'll know which one it is." He stood near the mast, hugging the boom with one arm as he focused a light beam on the fast approaching buoy. "*Yee-ha!* Number 207! We're home free!"

From there, Marcie and Ed put their absolute faith in the GPS map to guide the boat to the south end of Hog Hill Island. At first it looked like a gray lump on the horizon, visible only when lightning flashed in the distance. As the gray lump grew larger, a dim light seemed to wink on and off above it.

Soon they were close enough to see waves crashing into the trees on the shoreline. Ed took over manning the motor and Marcie grabbed a long pole and stood on the deck near the bow. She focused a flashlight beam on the trees. She was looking for something. They had done this before.

"Cut it!" Marcie shouted.

The motor suddenly throttled back and stopped. The waves decreased slightly as the boat entered the protected side of the island, away from the wind. They drifted with the cresting water toward the tangled growth of mangrove trees. It looked as if they were going to crash right into them.

Ed shoved a white, rubber bumper at Elbow. "Here, put this over the side when you see we're about to hit something," he ordered, then manned the other side as Marcie took the bow.

Elbow did as he was told. It was damn hard to see anything in the dark. They passed a sign. A flash of lightning illuminated it. 'WARNING - VIPERS. *Yikes!* Not again! Elbow thought he was done with snakes.

Mangrove branches came at him from all angles, screeching along the hull of the boat and hitting him in the face and arms. Waves moved the boat up and down. What the hell were they doing? Was there really a passage through these things? No wonder the boat needed patching if they did this on a regular basis.

The screeching noise stopped as the boat slid into a small, calmer canal along the shoreline. Although waves still crashed into the waterside mangrove trees, the trees inside the canal were relatively well protected. The boat was safe. They were safe. Elbow wanted to get off the boat and kiss a mangrove.

Ed arranged the bumpers while Marcie tied up the boat. They worked together to undo some mechanism to release the mast, then lowered it carefully to a sort of brace above the motor. Next they brought out an old army camouflage net and draped the entire boat with it. The mast and boat would be invisible in the mangroves if anyone sailed past or even flew over it.

What the hell did they need to hide? It was certainly overkill if they were just seeking shelter during a storm or even trespassing. Elbow reasoned it was none of his business. He had done a bit of camouflage on occasion himself, but drugs or guns were not something he messed with. He had his standards. Borrowing a motor bike now and then and freeing an avocado from a tree in someone's yard was about far as he went. Using abandoned garden sheds or old warehouses to live in wasn't really stealing. He thought of it as efficient recycling.

Ed arranged a wooden plank to shore on one side of the deck, crossed it, and disappeared into the underbrush.

"Where is he going?" Elbow asked.

"Oh, just to check on a few things," Marcie told him. "I'm going to see how bad it is on the other side of the island. You stay here and sleep if you can. You didn't get a rest break." She kissed him on the cheek. "You did a great job. We're safe here for now."

Elbow watched her slip over the side onto the embankment and disappear into the dark. She was right. He was tired. He opened the hatch and went below into the cabin. It was dark. He removed the yellow rain poncho and stripped off his wet clothes and shoes. Man, what a night. No sleep, waves crashing, wind howling, and he couldn't even look at the beer. He was beat. He laid down on the bunk. It was damp. What the hell, he was tired enough to sleep on the flooded deck.

The hatch clicked open again. Elbow opened one eye. It was Marcie. She left the hatch open just a sliver to let in some air. She had her back to him. He watched as she peeled off her tee shirt and shorts. Oh my, she was fine indeed! She turned around, looked at him, smiled, and climbed into his bunk next to him. Suddenly he wasn't nearly as tired as he was before.

CHAPTER 8: STILL WATERS

Elbow slowly opened one eye and then the other. Where the hell was he? A thin shaft of light illuminated the room. It smelled damp and musty. There was another smell too, besides the wet and mold. It was vaguely familiar, sweet and sour at the same time.

He couldn't quite focus. He stretched his arms and bumped into wood. The space was narrow, claustrophobic. He fleetingly thought of a coffin. It was the boat. He was in the cabin of the boat.

Marcie! He lay back on the pillow. How could he forget Marcie? It was a great night! How in the world did they manage in that tiny bunk? Where was she?

He climbed out of the bunk, retrieved his plastic bag and dressed in relatively dry clothes. Real, honest to goodness sunlight was shining through the slightly open hatch. Was it the eye of the hurricane, or did the storm somehow pass farther east and run out to sea?

He pushed the hatch open and climbed out on deck. He could hear waves washing up against the outer edge of the mangroves, but it was calm in the small channel where the boat was moored.

The sweet and sour smell was slightly more intense on deck. Where was everyone? He negotiated the small plank at the side of the boat and stepped onto dry land. His legs and body still reacted to the rocking motion of the boat even though he was on solid ground. It was almost as annoying as walking drunk.

A narrow path cut through the tall grass. He followed it up an embankment to a thicket of trees. A house made of vines and branches was barely visible inside the tangle. Camouflage just like the boat? A small opening in the brush allowed just enough room to wiggle through a sort of doorway. Inside it was dark.

"Anyone here?" He asked.

"Shut him up!" Ed whispered.

Marcie grabbed his arm and pushed him against the wall of vines. "Shh! Be quiet."

"What's with all the secrecy?" He whispered.

"Shh!" She said and put her hand over his mouth.

Then Elbow heard it. The faint throb of a motor. It grew louder and louder. Marcie held her breath. The sound moved on past the mangroves, decreased in pitch and volume and disappeared as quickly as it came.

Marcie took her hand away from his mouth and backed up to release him. "Sorry about that."

"I'm not," Elbow said and smiled. They enjoyed the moment.

"Don't ever do that again," Ed told him. "We got enough problems without someone snooping and seeing us here."

"Sorry."

"He's okay, Pa. He saved the motor didn't he? Maybe we should show him."

Ed gave him a real hard look then nodded his head. "You breathe a word of this to anyone, and the sharks will have you for breakfast. You got that?"

"Yes sir," Elbow mumbled.

Marcie rolled her eyes. "Knock off the drama, will you, Dad? I told you he's okay."

Marcie took Elbow's hand and led him out the doorway. She stopped and listened in all directions. She whispered. "We don't talk too much outside. You hear a motor, you just tap me on the shoulder and we'll just hunker down and be invisible, understand?"

Elbow nodded his head. What was this? Were they poachers, Mafia hit men, bank robbers, or what? Marcie skirted around the side of the house into the dense undergrowth. It got darker and denser. Elbow started fending off low branches and suddenly they were standing in a small clearing with a perfect canopy of leaves above them, shielded from the sky. The sweet/ sour smell was strong. Then it dawned on him.

He had smelled something like it before, under the pool tables at the Shark's Nest, after drinks got spilled and soaked into the floor boards. It was a still. Marcie and her dad had a still. They were moonshiners!

Marcie found an almost invisible opening in the tangled thicket at the edge of the clearing and motioned for him to follow her. Small trees around at the edge had been bent and tied together at the top to form a sort of roof. There it was, a small still, in all its shining, copper glory. Rather than a fire under the bottom, there was a hot plate. The still was running with a small, steady drip of clear liquid coming out into gallon jugs.

"Pretty slick operation. How the heck do you plug it in?" Elbow asked.

"We sort of tapped into the solar panel for the navigation light on top of the island. They come like clockwork a couple of times a year to check on it, so we just run it between times. People don't come here much because of the VIPER signs."

"Are there really snakes?"

"Hell no. We just put up the signs to discourage visitors. Works like a charm. People hate snakes."

"Yeah, I'm one of them. The mash smell is pretty strong. What do you do with that?"

"Depends on how much there is. Sometimes we bury it, but too much in one place kills the trees. Sometimes we mix it with sea water to kill off the yeast and stuff, then we go for a little night sail and dump it in small batches in the ocean."

"Is there much of a market for moonshine?"

"Heck yes. We could sell a ton of it, but you gotta watch out all the time. They're looking for operations like this. That's why we got to be doubly careful. Want to taste some? Just run your finger under the drip over there."

Elbow wetted his finger in the clear liquid and lifted it to his mouth. He blinked his eyes. The buzz from just that tiny sample was instant. "*Whoo!* Smooth!"

CHAPTER 9: ESCAPE PLAN

Ed joined them in the enclosure. Elbow could feel his scathing look as he grabbed the front of his shirt. "You breathe even one word, ONE WORD, about this and I'll be dumping you out at sea along with the mash!"

"Yeah, sure. I'm not a stool pigeon. I'm allergic to cops. Um...You're wrinkling my lapels."

Ed let go of his shirt, tapped the side of the still, and checked the flow. "Someone will probably be out to check the light at the top of the hill after the hurricane. The sooner we get everything out of here the better. The still is almost done running. We'll go for a delivery tonight and dump some mash on the way. You and Elbow-boy here can load the plastic bags of mash and carry them to the boat."

Marcie made a face. "My least favorite thing. It stinks."

Ed capped up the gallon jug under the drip and put another in its place. Another hard look came Elbow's way as Ed disappeared outside with several full gallon jugs under his arm.

"We better double bag everything so it doesn't spill on the way to the boat or worse, in the boat," Marcie said.

"This stuff could get heavy."

"Yeah. Don't put more in each bag than you are willing to carry. We already mixed it with sea water but it still stinks."

"Why is your dad so angry? I'm not going to blab to the cops."

"He's like that all the time. I'm gettin' real tired of it too. Man, he thinks I'm his drudge slave. I'm thinking of abandoning ship the next chance I get. You know, just disappearing when he makes a delivery."

"I could help you if you want. I don't exactly fancy a career as a bootlegger."

She looked around, then whispered. "Tonight? You really would? Tonight?"

"Sure," he whispered back. "I would have to scout out the scene a little bit wherever we're going, but we could try. If it's not good we can try again some other night."

"We have to do more than try. He's mean when people cross him."

"We have to be real secret then."

"Can I bring my stuff?" she asked.

"We can't be weighed down with a lot of stuff," he said. "If there's not too much, put it in one of the bags like these, and we'll hide it among the bags of mash. By the way, where are we going?"

"Well, not to Flamingo, that's for sure. It's just the headquarters of the Everglades park there. Probably someplace farther up the coast toward Miami. There seem to be a lot of thirsty folks in that direction."

Elbow smiled at her. "You were making a delivery in Key West before the storm, weren't you?"

"Yes."

He smiled again. They finished filling the plastic bags, carried them carefully to the sailboat and stored them below deck in the cabin.

"Come with me to get my stuff. It's not much, but if my dad's there we'll have to be real quiet."

They returned to the camouflaged house. Marcie held up her hand to stop Elbow before they went through the opening. "Listen," she whispered and laughed. "He's snoring. He sampled the hootch. He won't be awake until at least four or five o'clock this afternoon."

"It's really strong stuff. You sure he'll even wake up then?" Elbow asked.

"Yeah, that's why he was so grumpy yesterday. He didn't get his usual snort."

"Maybe we should beat it now while he's asleep."

"We could, but not with the sailboat. He would kill me if I took it."

"I'm pretty good at getting lost and staying lost."

She smiled at him. "I'll bet you are. I'm ready to do almost anything to get off this island and stay lost." She thought for a moment. "We could inflate the dinghy and sort of 'borrow' the electric motor. It would get us as far as the mainland. I could never do it by myself."

"I'm in. What do we do?"

"You stay here. I'll go inside and get my stuff."

Elbow looked around at the brush and vines that covered the makeshift house. All in all it was pretty slick, something that he might think to do himself if the need ever arose. The only problem would be bugs and critters and even snakes that might want to take up residence in it too. He shuddered.

Getting back to civilization would be a good idea. There were people in Miami he might want to avoid, but there were other places a fellow could relax and enjoy things without getting arrested.

CHAPTER 10: HIDE AND SEEK

The inflatable dinghy was stored in a compartment under the floor of the sailboat cockpit. It was a struggle to lift it out of the tight space and carry it off the boat.

"I'm glad I didn't know your emergency boat was packed in there so tight. It would take half an hour to remove it in an emergency," Elbow told her.

"We need to blow it up too," Marcie reminded him. "But we have to carry it over to the other side of the island before we do that."

"Why?"

"Because it won't fit through the path and the trees all blown up. And if we do it here, Dad might see us."

"Good plan."

They marched through the tall grass and thickets carrying the black, rubber raft on their heads safari style. They passed the signal light at the top of the small hill and negotiated the path down to a wooden pier.

Marcie pointed to the thin strip on gray on the horizon. "That's the mainland. I often come here and just look at it. So near yet so far," she said wistfully.

"Okay, how do we inflate this thing?" Elbow asked.

Marcie laid the dinghy out on the grass behind some mangroves. Folded up inside was a small bellows. She attached it to the boat and began pumping it with her foot.

"Here let me do that," Elbow volunteered. "You go back and get the motor and our stuff."

"The electric motor takes two people to carry with the battery and all. Leave the dinghy until we get back. We better hurry."

She folded up the dinghy so it wouldn't be seen. They retraced their steps back to the sailboat. They were about to step on board when Marcie stopped and pulled Elbow down into the tall grass.

"Damn, he's awake," she whispered. "He's on the boat. Did I remember to close the dinghy hatch? If he sees it open he will kill me for sure."

"It was closed," Elbow whispered. "I remember because I stepped on it trying to lift the dinghy on my head."

"Thank God."

They settled into the grass and watched Ed pack his precious alcohol containers inside the rear seats. Ed took a look around and checked the cabin to make sure the mash bags were properly stored. On deck again, he closed the hatch and locked it. He turned toward the open water beyond the mangroves and stood still, listening. Satisfied, he climbed off the boat and headed back to the vine house.

"Quick," Marcie said. "We need to get the motor and the battery before it gets dark. He'll be back then."

Elbow followed as she boarded the boat and unscrewed the electric motor and detached the cable to the battery in a side panel under the deck. She handed them both to him and motioned to hide them in the tall grass. He did as she asked and returned to the boat. He found her wriggling through a small vent hatch in front of the mast, trying to get into the cabin. "What the hell do you think you're doing? We got to get going and inflate the dinghy!"

"I'm not going without my stuff. He locked the cabin hatch!" She disappeared into the cabin.

Elbow secretly groaned. Soon the top of a plastic bag appeared, sticking out of the hatch. Elbow pulled on it. It popped out all at once, almost toppling him into the camouflage netting covering the boat.

"As long as you're there, get mine too. It's in the cabinet under the bunk."

A minute later another bag appeared at the hatch. It was a little bigger but softer in shape and required some pushing and pulling to get it through. Elbow quietly carried them both on shore and came back for Marcie.

She reached her hands up through the hatch. Elbow grabbed onto her wrists and lifted her up until her arms and shoulders were out.

"I'm stuck."

"Damn. Try turning a little sideways. That's how you went in."

This time she wiggled sideways and Elbow pulled her free. They closed the hatch and crossed the plank to dry land. She paused a moment to look at the boat.

"You changed your mind?" he asked.

"Hell no! Let's get out of here before he starts looking for us."

They divided the load evenly between them and took a longer route back to the pier to avoid Ed.

CHAPTER 11: CRABS

Marcie looked at the position of the sun in the sky. "We have about two hours of daylight left before sunset and maybe another forty-five minutes of twilight before Dad gets serious about looking for us. He likes to make runs at night. Key West was an exception because of the storm. You step on the bellows for a while, and then I'll take a turn. If we get the dinghy inflated, we might make it to the mainland before dark."

They worked for about an hour, taking turns. Elbow tired quickly. He realized lounging on the beach and putting back a few beers was not the best fitness regimen. Marcie took a turn. Elbow couldn't help but admire her physique and stamina. She smiled at him as he rested in the grass.

She stopped suddenly and looked up the hill. "Listen!" she whispered. "He's looking for us already. The rubber boat is only three-quarters filled. Help me get it into the water with all our stuff. The only place to hide it and us is under the pier."

They waded into the water, dragging the limp boat, the electric motor, battery and their two plastic bags behind them and eased it all under the low pier. Elbow felt something move across his feet and started squirming. "There's something crawling around down there," he whispered in panic.

"Horseshoe crabs. They won't bite," she whispered, putting her hand to his lips to indicate absolute silence. Elbow wasn't so sure the crabs knew they weren't supposed to bite. He endured the crab torture in silence.

Soon Ed's footsteps thudded above them on the pier. "Marcie!" He yelled in a hoarse whisper. "Damn that girl. She's off somewhere with that idiot. When I find her…" He tramped off the pier and headed back up the hill.

Marcie breathed a sigh of relief. "He's gone. Come on. Let's put a little more air in this thing and get out of here. He's really ticked off, but he won't be able to get the sailboat out of the canal very easily without the electric motor. That buys us a little time. But once he sees the motor is gone he'll figure it out and check for the dinghy. He'll be out for blood then."

They were soaking wet. Elbow stripped off his tee shirt and jeans. Marcie laughed. "Don't worry. We'll dry off pretty quick. "We might get wetter later on."

They dragged the squishy boat up onto the shore and worked to fill it with air. Finally they were ready. Marcie found a sturdy tree branch to attach the motor to so they could hold it over the side, then hooked up the battery. Elbow packed in the plastic bags and they were ready to launch.

Marcie's face showed a bit of panic. "Damn, I forgot the life preservers!"

"We can't go back for them now. We've come this far. I say we go."

She nodded. "Right. Let's launch!"

They pushed off from shore. A current took them eastward, away from the island. When they were a safe enough distance, Marcie used the electric motor to run diagonally across the current, toward the thin, gray stretch of mainland on the horizon. She turned and looked back at the island.

Elbow grinned. "Want to go back?"

"No! It's just that this place has been home for a while. It looks really small in the middle of all that water, doesn't it?"

"That's because it *is* small. The world is much bigger than a boat and a hunk of grass and trees."

"Yeah. I'll think of that when I get a tinge of homesickness."

Elbow stretched out in the bottom of the boat and rested his head on the side. "You ever try any of your dad's hooch?"

"Once. That was enough. That stuff is pure poison. I still can't fathom why people pay good money for it."

"Yeah, people who drink it are missing a few brain cells already." Elbow sat up in the dinghy and looked at the gray strip of mainland. "Is it my imagination or is the land getting farther away?"

"It's not your imagination. The current is strong here. It's muddy too, and there is a lot of stuff floating on the water because of the storm. Keep a look out. There is not much civilization along the coast until we get closer to Miami."

The sun set and a thin, crescent moon followed it into the sea. They were alone on the water in gathering darkness. The gray strip of mainland dissolved into the black night sky. No lights were visible as a million stars appeared above them.

"Wow!" Elbow said.

"You never saw the night sky before?" Marcie teased.

"Not like that. Too many lights or maybe I never looked. The only stars I know are the Big Dipper thing. But there are so many stars I can't even see that. Where is it?"

She pointed off to their left about halfway to the horizon.

"I'm impressed. You even know your way in the dark."

She smiled then suddenly turned. "Quiet. There's another boat off to the right running without lights." She swiveled the motor to turn the dinghy rapidly to the left.

Elbow strained to see the other boat in the darkness. It was pretty far away, but Marcie was taking no chances. She was headed for the safety of a small island of mangroves that looked like all the other little islands they passed. She skirted around to the far side and turned off the motor. The dinghy gently coasted to a stop on a small sandbar.

"We'll stay here until it passes," she whispered. "I hope it's not my dad, and I hope he didn't see us."

Elbow laid down in the bottom of the dinghy and pulled her down next to him. "Maybe we should just stay here for the night. You know, give the motor a rest." He could see her smile in the dim starlight. The night air was warm. Gentle waves lapped against the boat. They stayed.

CHAPTER 12: STRONG CURRENT

A thud on the side of the dinghy jolted Elbow and Marcie awake. The sky showed pink in the east. They could hear cars zipping along pavement above them. She sat up and looked. "Damn! It's the Keys causeway! Hurry, grab onto that concrete pillar before the current takes us into the shipping lane!"

"How did we get here?" He tried to stretch his arms around the pillar. "This thing is full of some kind of slime. It's hard to grab hold."

"It's low tide right now. Do the best you can while I get the motor hooked up and in the water. The tide must have set us free from the sand bar while we were asleep and we floated all night in the current. We could be near Key Largo."

"That's good isn't it?"

"Yeah, if my dad isn't there before us. It's one of his stops. We're lucky if he passed us in the night. He would maybe have chucked us out into the sea to swim for it. Okay, the motor is in the water. You can let go of the pillar now."

Elbow leaned over the side to wash the pillar goo off of his hands and arms.

"You might not want to go dragging your hands in the water like that. There might be sharks," Marcie advised.

"Sharks?"

"Yeah. They follow the Gulf Stream north this time of year."

He curled his fingers into tight balls and backed away from the water. "I don't know which I hate worse, snakes, gators, or sharks. And I'm not too fond of mosquitos and horseshoe crabs either."

"We should be all right in the boat. We'll head for the next island, whatever it is. There's less current and less boat traffic under the causeway and we can hide behind the pillars if we need to."

Elbow tried wiping the pillar goo off of his hands without touching the water.

Marcie scanned the water in all directions as they made their way under the causeway.

"You're really scared aren't you?" he said.

She looked at him but didn't answer.

Elbow let it drop. He had met a few guys like her dad. They were mean enough sober, but even meaner drunk. There were some things it was best not to pry into.

They reached a wide gap in the causeway pillars as the road above them arched up into a taller span for boat traffic to travel underneath.

"Keep a keen eye out here. We're going to cross against boat traffic and hug the mainland. The fast cigarette boats are hard to spot if they're going full out. All we have to get out of their way is this bitty motor." Marcie looked both ways and turned the motor to drive them out into the open expanse of water to head for the other side of the causeway bridge.

They were almost to the safety of the far set of pillars when a large ferry boat passed behind them. The wake threatened to swamp the dinghy, sending it whirling around in dizzy circles.

"The motor quit!" She fumbled with the battery cable. "Damn, it won't start. Must have caught some debris in the propeller. We're in the current again! Hold on!" Marcie yelled.

Elbow held on.

"Damn," Marcie swore. "We're getting farther away from the mainland shore! This current is a beast. Paddle with your hands or it might take us past Miami and out into the Atlantic."

"What about the sharks?"

"To hell with the sharks. Paddle!"

Elbow gritted his teeth, leaned over the side of the dinghy and scooped water with all his might. Marcie did the same on the opposite side. The rubber boat responded and headed toward the mangrove trees along the coast.

A final gentle wave washed them into the outer tangle of mangrove roots along the shore. Marcie grabbed hold of a protruding root. "You can rest now. We made it. We're safe."

Elbow rolled over. "Safe from what? My arms are burning, I'm thirsty. I'm hungry. And all we can see is mangroves."

Marcie reached for the plastic bag that held her stuff. "Here, I swiped a few bottles of beer and a bag of pretzels. Help yourself."

"Marcie, you are amazing!" Pretzels and beer. Marcie was a never ending source of amazement. It takes a special woman to think about bringing beer and pretzels in the middle of a desperate getaway.

"Give me a hand here, will you, Elbow? The waves are pushing us into the roots. If this dinghy gets punctured, we will be wallowing in sea water instead of pretzels and beer."

He could see her point. One glance down into the water he could see horseshoe crabs. Farther out there could be sharks. The beer could wait.

"There's water in the bottom. We've sprung a leak!" Marcie shouted. "The mangrove roots must have punctured it. Quick, see if you can find the hole and hold your hand over it."

Elbow tried to cover the hole with his hand to stop the flow. It was useless. Nothing stopped it. It squirted up like a fountain. The inflated ring around the outside was still sound, but the weight of the water pouring in made the dinghy a sluggish lump as it rode lower and lower in the water.

Marcie quickly slipped the electric motor and the battery into one of the plastic bags to keep them dry. "Push us away from the mangroves with the branch, Elbow. We can't risk poking a hole in the side of the dinghy! Damn, where are the boats when you need them," Marcie complained to the wind.

"We can't keep doing this forever," Elbow told her.

"Maybe we won't have to. Listen..." She put a hand to her ear. "I hear a motor."

They strained to hear. The steady drone of dual motors thrummed louder and louder. A pontoon boat slowly came into view filled with early morning anglers.

"Help" Marcie shouted. "Elbow, yell and wave your arms!"

Elbow rose up on his knees, waved his arms, and yelled. Marcie stood up and tried to do the same. Water poured over the sides of the unstable dinghy, filling it to the brim. Marcie tumbled into the water. The dinghy recoiled and catapulted Elbow out the other side.

"Help!" Marcie yelled, treading water, and waving her arms.

Elbow submerged and scrambled furiously with his arms, flaying wildly in every direction. He resurfaced, trying to breathe, desperately trying to grab onto the side of the dinghy. Marcie grabbed him by the back of his shirt and draped him over the side.

People in the pontoon boat started pointing in their direction. It turned and headed toward them. They crowded the front railing under the canopy. A sign on the bow said LEISURE PARADISE. It was a senior citizen excursion out for sightseeing or fishing.

Someone onboard shouted, "Ahoy there. Do you need help?"

"Yes, we sprang a leak," Marcie yelled back.

"Throw them a life preserver, Helga, then we'll reel them in."

Helga was a good shot and almost clobbered Elbow in the head with the orange life ring. He grabbed onto it and struggled to keep a hand on the dinghy too. Marcie grabbed both him and the dinghy. The senior citizens formed sort of a chain to pull on the rope to maneuver the dingy toward the boat.

Elbow scrambled onto one of the pontoons. Marcie followed him, trying to hold on to their plastic bags. The blades on the electric motor tore through the thin plastic, spilling some of Elbow's Salvation Army wardrobe into the water. He grabbed as much as he could and draped it in a clump over the pontoon.

A large woman in green shorts and a bright orange shirt with blue flowers on it, tossed around orders. "Ray and Oscar, give those two a hand with those bags. Wilma, step back a bit so they can get on board here. Helga, take that rope and tie that dinghy to the side before it gets any more holes in it. You two look a little bedraggled. Looks like we came along at just the right time."

Elbow coughed, trying to expel some of the water he swallowed when he submerged. The large lady grabbed his arm and hauled him over the railing. She gave him a swift slap on the back to help him catch his breath. The woman packed quite a wallop. He doubled over and stumbled into the opposite railing.

"There you go, buddy. You weren't out here during the hurricane were you? The ocean was pretty rough. That whole mess turned right out to sea before it did any major damage. My name's Selma. This here is Ambrose, the captain, and everybody else has a name tag."

"Glad to meet you," Elbow croaked. "Many thanks for the rescue. I'm Elbow and this is Marcie."

"Elbow? Is that your Christian name?" Selma asked.

"It's just my name."

"Where you from?"

"We're—"

"We're from Key West," Marcie said hurriedly. "We caught a ride up here with some guy, but he just dropped us off at Flamingo. We were tryin' to get to Miami."

Elbow observed Marcie was good at bending the truth when she needed to. Beer, pretzels, a secret moonshiner, and the occasional half-truth story, Marcie was a woman of sterling attributes. He was liking her more and more by the minute.

"Well, you just stick with us and we can get you back to Leisure Paradise, maybe find someone to take you the rest of the way." Selma told them.

"Leisure Paradise?"

"Yep. That's where we live." Wilma said. "It's a retirement place. Only double-wide trailers allowed. We even have our own bingo parlor. There is a craft room where we make stuff out of pine needles, and a couple of times a week we fire up the pontoon boat and go fishing." Wilma's eyes sparkled as she recited the wonders of her retirement village.

"Thanks for stopping. We were in a real pickle," Elbow said.

"It's our Christian duty and the law of the sea," Selma informed them.

Elbow suddenly wondered if they were a preachy bunch. If so, he thought he might prefer the peril of the wet dinghy to rescuing his wayward soul.

"Get these poor folks a towel, Ambrose. You two hungry? We got some sandwiches and a few beers," Oscar offered.

Beer! Elbow perked up. The day was looking better. Oscar handed them each a peanut butter sandwich, a bottle, and winked. Oh joy. It was non-alcoholic beer.

CHAPTER 14: LEISURE PARADISE

The fake beer was warm and the limp peanut butter sandwich tasted vaguely like fish bait, but a rescue was a rescue. Elbow smiled politely. Wilma sat down next to him and patted him on the knee with what he hoped was motherly concern. The pontoon boat made a wide, slow turn to head back in the opposite direction.

Elbow looked at Marcie. She looked up and winked. She had obviously made a hit with the retired men. They clustered around her, offering her more damp sandwiches.

Helga busied herself hanging Elbow's wet clothes on the railing. Although he appreciated the effort, he could have done without displaying his underwear, like flags fluttering in the breeze for all the world to see.

The pontoon boat droned at a steady snail's pace past monotonous miles of tangled mangroves. Finally, a long, low dock appeared along the shore, backed by a grove of palms. A sign announced LEISURE PARADISE in bold orange letters. A small strip of man-made beach completed the picture. Beyond the trees, there were glimpses of trailers with white roofs, baking in the sun.

The boat slowed to a crawl as it approached the pier. With a final reverse thrust it nudged the end of the pier and bumped to a stop. Captain Ambrose tied it up neatly, and the small army of pontoon anglers started moving the electric motor and plastic bags onto the pier.

Wilma collected Elbow's wardrobe. "They're a little damp, honey, but you can hang them up on my clothesline. The sun will dry them in no time." She smiled and patted his knee again. Wilma was the touchy-feely type.

Elbow made his way onto the pier. He was so grateful to set foot on dry land, he almost knelt down to kiss it. His swimming skills were less than stellar. He never wanted to advertise it, but he usually gave water a wide berth.

"Say, you two wouldn't be interested in earning a little money, would you?" Selma asked. We need someone to do cleanup and repair work and some help in the office. It even comes with a small trailer to live in. Nothing fancy but it's free."

Elbow thought about the soggy wad of cash tucked in his shoe. It wouldn't get him very far. He was usually allergic to work, but as long as the job didn't involve getting back on a boat, he wouldn't mind a bit of extra cash. Leisure Paradise might be as good a place as any for Marcie to hide out until the danger of her dad finding her passed.

Elbow looked around at the collection of double wide trailers neatly spaced down three streets. Coconuts and palm tree fronds were scattered everywhere on the pavement. The hurricane had been there, but it only rearranged some of the landscaping. There was a large cinder block building in the middle with BINGO in big orange letters above the door. A lone, gravel, access road stretched off straight into the low, swampy land at the end of the main street.

Marcie stood starring at the trailers. The look in her eyes said it all. We were rescued for this?

Elbow put his arm around her shoulders. "How bad can it be? We could stay here for a few weeks, earn some money and then split."

She gave him a weak smile. "Yeah, I can learn to make place mats out of palm fronds or knit doilies, maybe make a killing on bingo night."

"At least here you'd be safe from your dad and you won't have to sleep in a damp boat or a hut made out of vines. What do you say? You could help in the office and I could collect stray coconuts."

She shrugged her shoulders. "Yeah, okay. It's better than nothing. If we get desperate we can always repair the dinghy with duct tape and take our chances with the current and the mangroves again."

Selma was delighted to sign them up and show them around. The free trailer turned out to be a small aluminum thing up on blocks about six by ten feet. It was just big enough for a bed at one end and a bench to sit on at the other with a minuscule shower/toilet room in between. A shelf with a tiny sink served as the kitchen. It all smelled faintly of cats. Marcie wrinkled her nose and opened a window. Aside from the odor-de-cat, Elbow approved. It was a step up from the garden shed.

"Well, I'll leave you two to fix things up the way you want," Selma told them. "Just amble over to the office when you're ready and I'll get you started. The grounds got messed up a bit with the storm so there's lots to pick up. See you soon." With that she lumbered out the door.

"Man, I thought the boat was small," Marcie said. "This is like living in a tin can. I hope it doesn't leak."

"It's not the Ritz, but it's just for a couple of weeks. Unless you have a pile of money in your plastic bag, it will have to do. I got about twenty-three dollars in my shoe so we can buy some groceries and maybe a can of air freshener. I'm going to hang my stuff out to dry. We can put the mattress outside in the sun too and make it smell better."

They wrestled the mattress out the door and propped it up against the side of the trailer. They left the door and windows open to air out the inside. Elbow draped his damp clothes on the edge of the trailer roof and the branches of a nearby pine tree to dry.

Marcie took him aside. "I wasn't going to say anything on the boat, but you really don't know how to swim do you?"

"Ah, well, you know getting tossed like that out of the dinghy sort of like surprised me. But yeah, I never really got out of the *tadpole* group in junior high. I was really skinny and I couldn't stay on top of the water."

"And you got on a sailboat in the middle of the ocean and rode out a hurricane! You must be either crazy or desperate."

"I was kind of anxious to find a way out of Key West."

"Girl trouble or the cops?"

"Let's just say a change of scenery was a very good idea all the way around. At least it seemed like a good idea at the time."

She smiled. Simpatico.

Elbow guessed there were places she couldn't go back to either.

CHAPTER 15: ANTS AND COCONUTS

Marcie and Elbow spent a restless night. Their first night in the free trailer was hot and sticky with humidity. A small animal rustled outside underneath the window. Elbow hoped it wasn't a snake. Although the mattress was liberally sprayed with disinfectant, Lysol was not the most romantic fragrance. Mosquitos hummed at the window screens. Crickets and cicadas sang all night with their shrill, monotonous songs of courtship, love, and rejection. Morning came with a red sunrise, increased humidity and the promise of afternoon rain.

"Well, I'm off to the office to answer phones and make sandwiches," Marcie said as she trudged off to start her job.

"At least it's air conditioned," he yelled after her. "I'll be tooling around in the second hand golf cart with a wonky trailer on the back, picking up coconuts in the hot sun."

"I'll weave you a hat out of palm fronds!" She shot back.

Elbow began cleaning up the hurricane mess. It was hot, sweaty work. To amuse himself, he arranged the piles of coconuts artistically in a pyramid near the large pile of palm branches.

The entire Leisure Paradise compound was carved out of the swamp with construction debris. The land was raised only three feet above the surrounding water level. It all ended abruptly and descended into mangrove swamp at the edges. Elbow's predecessor used the swamp edge as a dump site for his trash collections. Elbow observed it formed a kind of barrier all around against wandering alligators.

Calls started coming into the office from several of the women to have Elbow drop by their trailers to change lightbulbs, sweep pine needles off trailer roofs and dispatch spiders from bathroom ceilings. The minute he stepped into Wilma Foley's trailer, he spotted the large birdcage in the corner of the living room. His track record was not good with birds, cockatoos in particular. This cage was owned by a rather large, agitated, gray parrot. As soon as he entered, it started a barrage of parrot insults at full volume. From the bird's reaction he figured there must be a secret bird network where he was listed as public enemy number one.

"Hush, you naughty bird." Wilma turned to Elbow and muttered, "He is such a noisy thing." Addressing the bird, she cooed, "But I *wuv* you, Dingo, don't I?" The bird ignored her and kept a beady bird eye on their human intruder.

Wilma wanted Elbow to help rearrange her living room furniture. It was heavy, Victorian stuff, surrounding a large electric organ that looked like it belonged in an old movie theatre. He managed to huff and puff his way through moving the organ and the hide-a-bed sofa. Dingo, the gray, feathered menace, took a few snaps at him when he got within range, but Elbow managed to stay clear of nipping distance.

Wilma insisted he stay afterwards and rest on the sofa. She offered him stale cookies and lukewarm iced tea while she sat next to him and patted his knee. He considered himself lucky to escape after only one cookie.

Sylvia Constantine wanted Elbow to get rid of a parade of ants that had invaded her kitchen. The fact that Sylvia left a veritable ant cornucopia out in the open on her counter top escaped her reasoning. She just wanted them gone.

Elbow followed the ant stream down to the kitchen floor and into a crack next to the refrigerator. Outside, he found their trail emerging from a small gap in the aluminum siding and followed it to a pile of debris near the edge of the swamp. If he burned the pile, he reasoned, the ants would burn too. Yeah, great plan.

He moved some fallen palm fronds to the top of the pile to stoke the fire nice and hot and lit it up. The palm fronds were crispy and roared with great enthusiasm, sending flames twenty feet up into the air. They ignited a near-by palm tree which dropped its entire load of coconuts into the burning pile where they exploded like bombs when the liquid inside turned to steam.

The ants were righteously enraged. Great masses of them emerged from the pile in all directions, carrying eggs, ready to fight. Elbow beat a hasty retreat back to Sylvia's trailer. She was in full defense mode when he arrived. The colony had somehow sent an ant email out to the scavenger group, and they clamped their little ant jaws into anything and everything. Sylvia was beating them off with a sponge mop in a vain attempt to stop their insane attack. Elbow grabbed her and hurried her out the door to the relative safety of the paved street.

"How the hell am I going to get them out of there now?" she asked. "They went crazy when that fire started!"

"Maybe you should stay out of there for a couple of days," Elbow said. "You know, let them calm down and move somewhere else. I'll plug the hole where they were getting in and you can put all the food they were after in plastic containers so maybe they will go somewhere else. They won't bother you anymore."

Sylvia narrowed her eyes and almost hit him with her sponge mop. "You don't know ants, do you, young man? I know ants! Now you got them all stirred up! Ants, being ants, will just hunker down, occupy another pile of debris, and regroup!"

They watched as the fire consumed the pile. The predicted afternoon rain shower reduced it to a charred, simmering lump.

CHAPTER 16: THE MARCIE SHOW

Life at Leisure Paradise settled into a routine. Elbow spent his days cutting grass and picking up debris from the streets. Residents regularly called the office with small jobs for him to do. Some called more than others.

Harriet Hoffmeyer's light bulbs seemed to need changing more than other residents. She always had yesterday's soggy coffee cake ready and wanted to talk when Elbow arrived.

Wilma "Knee Patter" Foley called quite often. She needed help at least once a week rearranging her living room. She usually called for help around three p.m. when it was hot and Elbow had his shirt off. She served him her special, rock-hard cookies and weak iced tea and always managed to sit next to him on the sofa and pat his knee.

Marcie's job was to sit in the air conditioned office, answer the phone and manage the small canteen/grocery store. It sold basic supplies like coffee, toilet paper, ready-made sandwiches, and soft drinks. There were a few tables both inside and out where residents could gather and be social.

On Tuesdays and Thursdays most of the ladies gathered in the craft room. They busied themselves talking and making dollhouse furniture out of beer cans. Some days they stitched pine needles together to make purses. On Friday night there was the social and entertainment highlight of the week, a potluck supper followed by music and the ever popular bingo tournament. Selma usually called the numbers, but attendance doubled when Marcie called them.

After Marcie cleaned up the canteen every day, she always went for a swim. It was the event of the day, each day, when Marcie arrived at the beach in the late afternoon in her bikini. The pier crowded up with men who were somehow keen to fish at that particular time of day.

Elbow caught the Marcie show one afternoon. He observed how she made the most of it, taking her time arranging her towel and taking off her shoes, before slowly strolling into the water. After a few lazy laps of the breast stroke and a couple of acrobatic dives to the bottom, she emerged from the sea and strolled casually back to her shoes and towel to dry off. Her red hair glistened in the sun as she shook it playfully to rub it with the towel. All fishing stopped as she bent over to fasten her sandals. Then she gave the pier a wave as she turned to walk way.

Late one particularly hot day, Elbow had just finished sweeping pine needles off Agnes Butterman's trailer roof. He was hot and sweaty. In spite of his aversion to water, he kicked off his tennis shoes and ran full tilt into the cool ocean behind Marcie. She squealed with delight and dived under the surface, playfully pulling him down too.

There was quite a drop off where the man-made beach ended and the bottom sloped steeply away into deeper water. Not being any kind of swimmer, Elbow scrambled wildly for the surface, coughing and gasping for air. Marcie neatly laid him out on his back with a lifesaver's arm around his neck and pulled him to shallower water where he could stand up.

"Sorry, honey, I forgot you can't really swim," she told him. "Are you okay?"

He coughed and spit out some water. "Yeah, fine, just great," he squeaked.

"Maybe I should teach you how to swim," she said as she tugged at his tee shirt and sank back down into the water. She motioned for him to follow her. He removed his tee shirt and tossed it up onto the beach.

"Now you just relax." She gently pressed her hands along his back lowering him into the water and supporting him to float. "There, you see. It's just like layin' down on a sofa." She let her legs stretch out underneath him. Her hands and body were doing more than just holding him up.

Elbow's eyes almost rolled back in his head. He had no idea swimming could be so... *sensual*. He made the mistake of relaxing so completely, that before he knew it, his head sank and he inhaled a snootful of water. He struggled to stand up, coughing and reaching for the sky and finally crawled onto the beach and sneezed water out his nose.

The men on the pier applauded. Elbow gave them a wave that didn't include too many fingers.

"Oh dear," Marcie said, "you okay?"

Elbow nodded his head and struggled to put on his sand-covered tee shirt as he staggered back to the trailer.

Later that night, Marcie was full of apologies. "I'm real sorry about the swimming lesson today, Elbow. Maybe I should teach you a few swimming moves on dry land first, so you can get a feel for it before you go in the water again."

He shook his head. "I'm not going back in that water for any reason. Maybe I won't take a shower or get too near a garden hose or even drink it either."

Marcie lay down on the bed. "Here, hon. You just come over here and I'll show you." She patted the bed next to her.

Elbow relented and lay down next to her, but none of her moves would ever keep anyone afloat in the water.

CHAPTER 17: SAUERKRAUT

Marcie was always in a good mood after they received their pay envelopes. "A few more of these we can think of getting out of here," she told Elbow.

"What? You don't like the deluxe accommodations? Or the peanut gallery on the pier when you go for a swim?" He teased.

"You can stay here and grow mold on your flip-flops like these dinosaurs, but I crave a little more fun than Friday night bingo."

"Yeah, I'm beginning to get the itch too. Some of the old dears are all right, but I could do without playing patty-cake with Wilma "Fingers" Foley or eating stale coffee cake with Harriet Hoffmeyer. Her kitchen always smells like vinegar or salad dressing."

"Victor's no picnic either. He comes into the canteen every day exactly at three o'clock and buys an ice cream sandwich. You could set your watch by him. Then he sits at the table near the office door and stares at me as he eats his ice cream sandwich until the ice cream gets soft and dribbles on his shirt."

"Want me to have a little conversation with him?"

"No. I can handle it. I'll move the tables or close the office door," she said. "In a couple of weeks we can plan our exit. The guy who delivers the soft drinks is pretty friendly. I can chat him up and see if he'll take us as far as that grocery store in the mall at the junction with the highway. From there maybe hitch a ride to Miami or anywhere else." Marcie's eyes lit up and she smiled. "Miami. I daydream about it. Maybe even go as far north as Orlando and get a job at Disney."

"Yeah, you could be Minnie Mouse," he said.

"And you can be Goofy."

"The possibilities are endless as long as there isn't a job picking up coconuts! I'm beginning to hate coconuts. And speaking of the little devils, I have to collect today's load and hurl them into the swamp.

Maybe I'll get lucky and hit a gator. See you." He gave her a kiss on the cheek and drove off in the golf cart.

Spotty rain showers descended in the afternoon. Elbow worked inside trying to unplug a toilet in Harriet Hoffmeyer's trailer. The job was made even harder by Mrs. Hoffmeyer's lap dog. Pooky was half Pomeranian and half pug, and not the most attractive parts of either one. He insisted on bringing balls into the small bathroom and dropping them in the toilet. He barked with a shrill, insistent demand to play the game that, in his minuscule brain, somehow included the toilet.

After the tenth wet ball in the toilet, Elbow picked up the over-active Pooky and shut him in the cabinet under the sink. The dog barked non-stop, but at least he could get on with unplugging the toilet.

It was one stubborn toilet. Elbow was sure it was stuffed with Pooky balls. He was ready to drop a cherry bomb down there to get it to move, but as a last resort he threaded a garden hose through the bathroom window sticking it as far as he could into the bottom of the toilet. He closed up the bathroom sink and shower drain and turned on the outside faucet full volume.

At first there was nothing, only the sound of water rushing in the hose. The dog stopped barking. That was either a good thing or a bad thing. Then it started howling, a mournful, sort of desperate, sound. Elbow opened the under sink cabinet. The dog sailed out the bathroom door, managed to get through the trailer screen door and whimpered at Mrs. Hoffmeyer's feet.

Then Elbow heard the same thing the dog did, a high-pitched hiss, then a sort of rattle, and finally, there was an explosion of pressure somewhere. The toilet gave a gulping, sucking sound as all the water in the bowl suddenly, violently, disappeared.

Someone screamed. Elbow rushed outside. Harriet and Pooky stood on the patio covered in sauerkraut. Strings of sauerkraut dripped over the edge of the roof and draped like garlands on the lawn chairs. It had all exploded out the vent stack on top of the trailer.

Elbow tried desperately to control the urge to laugh. Harriet did not find it at all amusing. There is nothing like being covered in old sauerkraut to make your sense of humor evaporate. She kept screaming.

Pooky was in seventh heaven, staring at the five or six brightly colored balls that had magically dropped out of the sky onto the patio along with the sauerkraut. He started eating clumps of the kraut with great gusto. The little howler was going to have one heck of a tummy ache later. Elbow almost suggested he could spray Mrs. Hoffmeyer and Pooky down with the garden hose but thought better of it.

"What did you do?" she demanded.

"The system must have been clogged up with that cabbage stuff. You know, the septic system couldn't take it and BLAM! it all came out the top." He tried to sound convincing like he really knew what happened.

That put a wave of fear into Harriet as she tried to wipe sticky strands of sauerkraut from her housedress. "You think it's safe to go back in the bathroom?" She asked.

"Sure, sure. It will probably be good for a day or so, but maybe you should hire a plumber to root it all out just to be safe."

She nodded her head and wobbled a bit as she mounted the steps into her trailer. Elbow hosed down the top of the trailer and the lawn chairs, then disappeared to the opposite end of the retirement compound. Experience taught him never to stay too close to disaster scenes, especially if he might have had something to do with the disaster.

CHAPTER 18: DOUBLE BINGO

Friday was bingo night. The ladies put on their best sixties makeup, formal sweat pants, flowered tops and a dose (or two) of perfume. The men seemed to think checkered shirts and straw hats were the proper attire to impress the ladies, suspenders optional.

This Friday, the potluck theme was Ethnic Specialties. People were encouraged to bring dishes from their family backgrounds. Elbow looked around at the spread of food on the buffet table, each dish labeled with the country it represented.

He whispered to Marcie as they made their way through the serving line. "I never knew stuffed cabbage was the national dish of so many countries. Considering my close encounter with cabbage recently, I think I'll take a pass on the *gawumpki*, or whatever that is, and go for baked beans and some mac and cheese, and wash it down with a beer."

"Gourmet dining at its finest," Marcie whispered back. "At least it beats noodle soup and crackers. That's about all we can manage to fix in that tiny trailer kitchen. I'm almost starting to look forward to the potluck bingo nights. It is definitely time to move on."

Many of the ladies insisted Elbow try their desserts. *No* was not an acceptable response. Helen Feldman served him a large slice of her apple strudel directly on top of Ruth Manchester's cherry tart and winked at him as she topped it with an extra-large dollop of whipped cream. Ruth was not pleased and a little hissy fit ensued. Selma, the manager, had to come out of the office to settle things down, and the two women took pains to sit on opposite sides of the room.

When the paper plates and plastic utensils were cleared away, Selma played music from the forties and fifties for *Dance Time*. Elbow sat back to observe the dancing styles of the Leisure Paradise Fred and Ginger duos. It was a mixed bag, more like the Flintstones wrestle Big Bird, but he had to give them points for enthusiasm.

The polka seemed to be a big hit. One of the men swooped Marcie around the polished linoleum floor and almost lost her with an surprise twirl at the end. Elbow laughed and Marcie returned the favor when Wilma Foley claimed a turn on the floor with Elbow. She was having the time of her life as she tried to turn a calypso number into a bump dance. She was a very energetic bumper.

When everyone had enough cardiac exercise, it was time for bingo. The group was serious about their Bingo, buying cards and setting them up in individual patterns that would mystically guarantee a winner. Their markers were poised and ready. Elbow was assigned to pick the numbers out of the cage.

Selma whispered a little advice before Marcie read off the numbers. "Now remember, dear, these folks are sometimes a little challenged with their eyesight and hearing. Be sure to say it loud and clear."

Marcie nodded. Elbow turned the cage and picked a number. Marcie announced it and punched the letters and numbers into a keyboard to display them on a big screen near the ceiling. Everything went smoothly for a few minutes, everyone concentrating intently on their numbers.

Marcie called "B10."

"Bingo!" Someone shouted. The room let out a collective "Ohh" of disappointment.

Selma stood and pointed. "Emily McGrath, you do that every week! Marcie's only read off six numbers. You either have the luckiest card in all of bingo or your marker has been playing bingo all by itself again! Somebody check her card, please."

Someone checked. Emily had playfully drawn circles around some numbers and connected the rest with a wavy line. She let out a giggle.

"Okay, everyone, false alarm," Selma told them. "Keep your cards. We'll just keep going."

Twenty numbers later, a real winner emerged. An hour later they played the final game, Double Bingo, with a grand prize of $150. All the numbers on a card had to be filled to win. Competition was fierce. Some residents had several cards reserved just for the final game. The room grew quiet. Big money was involved. This was serious business.

Elbow twirled the number cage around twice, opened the door at the top, and reached inside for the first number. Marcie read it off and made the sign, near the ceiling, blink on to display it. With every number, the only sound was the occasional squeaking of magic markers as the lucky few filled in or crossed off the precious squares.

The hand on the clock above the office door marched steadily around the dial counting off the seconds. Seconds turned into minutes until finally, Oscar Martin raised his cane and shouted, "BINGO!"

"He won last week too!" someone said.

"It's rigged!" came another shout.

"Now, now, don't everyone get all tied up in a knot," Selma said. "He has just as much chance as everyone else."

"Somebody messed with those number balls!"

"Check his card. Maybe it's a trick card!"

The crowd was getting a little surly. Selma checked the card and confirmed the winning numbers. Oscar shuffled up to the front of the hall to claim his money and did a little circle around his cane as a dance of joy. It did not endear him to the rest of the group. There were words of discontent as everyone left the Bingo hall.

"Wow everyone sure got upset about the Double Bingo prize," Marcie said. "They take their bingo seriously around here." She gave Elbow a kiss on the cheek. "Well...I'm off. Good night, hon."

Elbow looked as she went out the door. She gave him a little wave. My, that was sweet. He stayed to clean the tables, reset the chairs and sweep the floor. It had been a long day. He was tired. He muttered to himself as he hauled out the heavy trash bags. "This is beginning to feel like a real job. The sooner I get out of here and get to civilization, the better I'll like it."

As he approached the dumpster, five sets of red eyes stared at him out of the darkness. Raccoons out for a midnight snack.

"What the hell. Here you are, you masked bandits. Two big bags of delightful stuffed cabbage and leftover strudel. *Bon appetite!* Enjoy! I'm too tired to argue with you tonight. Try not to spread it around too much. I'm the guy who has to clean it up tomorrow. Listen to me. I'm talking to raccoons. I must really be tired."

He trudged back to the trailer. Marcie didn't even leave the light on for him. She was probably tired too. He took off his shoes and fell into bed.

CHAPTER 19: GETTING OUT

Saturday morning dawned bright and clear. Elbow rolled over in bed and winced as a ray of sunlight hit him in the eye. What time was it? Where the heck was Marcie? She usually gave him a nudge to get him up and get going. He sat up. He'd slept in his clothes again. They were all wrinkled. Marcie would cluck at him for that.

He got himself vertical and wandered a few steps to the kitchen at the front of the trailer. Marcie wasn't there. Something wasn't right. Maybe she was taking a morning swim.

Then he saw it. The row of hooks where she hung her clothes. They were all empty. She was gone. Sometime after bingo or during the night she just up and left. There was no note or anything.

He should have seen it sooner. Marcie's mind was always fixed on something else, getting away from her dad and doing something more with her life. Working in a leisure retirement village on the edge of nowhere just wasn't it. But sneaking off in the middle of the night was dirty pool, not that he hadn't done it himself a few times, but even so.

He stood up. His stash! He rummaged frantically in the kitchen where he hid it behind the instant coffee. Marcie never drank coffee. Gone! The whole thing gone! She didn't even leave him enough for a beer.

Served him right for trusting her, but damn it, he was always straight with her, sort of. I mean he never really told her a lie or anything. A guy has a right to his secrets and some things, like former girlfriends, you just don't share with your current girlfriend.

Damn!

Well, if she got out, maybe it was time for him to get out too. Somehow, another day pulling hooks out of fish for ladies on the pier, sweeping pine needles off trailer roofs and fighting raccoons over the garbage had lost its charm. Time to go. The old dears could sweep their own damn pine needles. He wouldn't miss Mrs. "Patty Cake" Foley's wandering hands even if she did slip him a fiver now and then. He had his standards, thin as they were.

How to get out, that was the trick. Money was the big problem. He would have to wait until after the next payday on Friday. The trouble was that Leisure Paradise was a long way from civilization with limited transport. The bi-weekly fishing expedition on the pontoon boat always ran in the opposite direction from Miami so that was out. The weekly bus to the mall up at the highway only ran on Thursdays so that would mean waiting almost two weeks to leave. There were always the delivery trucks. Maybe they wouldn't mind a passenger. He could help unload pop cans and nacho chips, but they only came on Wednesday so he would still have to wait until after payday.

Man, when you get an idea in your head like leaving, it just sticks there like gum on your shoe. One more round of moving heavy furniture and chucking coconuts to endure, oh joy.

The week passed slowly. The raccoons, emboldened by the heavy load of Friday night cabbage, made regular raids on the compound dumpster and garbage cans. Complaints started coming into the office.

"Elbow, these darn raccoons are gettin' to be a nuisance," Selma told him. "Some of them are even comin' in the trailers to raid the pet food bowls. And they made a mess of the dumpster. You know anything about that?"

"No ma'am," he lied.

"We can't have it. Those critters are a menace. Rabies and everything! See if you can lock those dumpsters down tighter. If that doesn't work, we'll just have to post a guard at night to scare 'em off."

Elbow knew who that guard would be. Great, just what he wanted to do, sit up all night and guard dumpsters and then sling coconuts during the day. Yet another reason to get out.

Midweek, Ted Olsen hired Elbow to paint the roof of his trailer. Ted was a retired painter with a bad hip. He no longer climbed ladders.

He sat in a lawn chair in the shade of his patio to critique every brush stroke Elbow laid down.

Besides the constant chatter from Ted, the sun was mercilessly hot. The bright aluminum paint reflected it double. Elbow felt like a slice of bread in a toaster, getting fried from both sides. The paint did not dry quickly but stayed sticky in the hot sun. The trailer roof got painted, but so did Elbow. How paint could get on the back of his shirt, cover his shoes and decorate his hair was a mystery. Ted found it amusing.

Elbow almost had to bathe in turpentine to remove the paint. His shirt was a total loss. He painted his shoes solid aluminum to disguise the slop. They were his only pair and it made them stiff. The smell of oil paint and turpentine lingered. He avoided anything with an open flame for two days for fear his shoes or hair would ignite.

There was one more round of furniture wrestling at Wilma Foley's. Dingo, her parrot, was on full alert. So far Elbow had managed to escape being bitten. But this time the bird sized up the situation and finally made its move, clipping Elbow neatly on the ear as he grunted past, moving Mrs. Foley's three-ton organ. It bled like a fountain.

Wilma was in a tizzy. "Oh no! Don't get that blood on the sofa!" she screamed. "You naughty bird. Mommy told you not to bite people."

Elbow left twenty dollars richer. "Well, that damn bird was finally good for something," he muttered to himself as he pocketed the twenty and taped a bandage on the top of his ear. "I'll have to throw this shirt away too. At this rate I won't have to pack anything when I finally get the hell out of here."

CHAPTER 20: BINGO BASH

Friday finally arrived. Elbow felt flush with his pay, the twenty from Wilma and the hundred Ted Olsen paid him for the trailer roof paint job. He tucked it firmly in his aluminum-painted sneakers. All he needed now was transportation, and *zip* he'd be gone. Something was bound to turn up. He could feel it in his bones.

As luck would have it, a couple guys with a rental truck showed up late in the afternoon to clean out Wilma Foley's trailer for a move to another retirement village north of Miami. The family resemblance was strong, maybe her sons. They were a bit paunchy and enjoyed quite a few beer breaks. Elbow didn't envy them the task of getting that organ and sofa out the door and into the truck. Dingo, the wonder parrot, would keep them busy too. It might even be fun to watch.

Loading the truck went slowly. Elbow kept an eye on it as he busied himself around the compound. The truck was his golden opportunity to get away and he wasn't going to miss it. The two sons stayed for the Friday night, potluck supper and bingo too. Wilma was both giddy and weepy as she sat with her friends.

Selma put Elbow in charge of the bingo ball cage again to draw the numbers while she took Marcie's place reading them off. Elbow wanted to be done and gone. He was itchy as he reached into the cage to pull out the numbers. The first few games went smoothly enough. It was the third game that got everyone riled up.

When Oscar Martin yelled "BINGO!" again, the place erupted in a collective complaint.

"He should be disqualified," someone shouted. "He won the big jackpot twice already!"

"Not fair!"

"What is this? Does he own the balls?"

"Someone needs to check those balls."

The group certainly took their bingo seriously. Selma quickly restored order, but the group was not pleased. Elbow could feel it in the air. If Oscar claimed another prize, there might be a full revolt.

Everyone settled back in. Oscar remained silent, and an uneasy peace was restored. The room grew quiet as everyone concentrated.

The big double bingo jackpot was the last game of the evening. After that, Elbow was ready to go. He almost twitched with anticipation. Freedom was so close.

The game started easily enough. As the numbers began to fill up the viewing screen near the ceiling, a few players gave Oscar an unsettled glance to make sure he stayed seated. Twenty five numbers were called. It was rapidly approaching the tipping point. Still no winner. The air was heavy with murmurs of exasperation and anticipation.

Elbow reached into the bottom of the ball cage. His shirt caught the top of the latched opening. He struggled to free himself. The cage lifted off the stand, turned upside down, and spilled the remaining balls onto the linoleum floor. They bounced and scattered across the floor and hid between the chairs under the tables.

The room gasped. Several players were agonizingly close to a winner. For a moment no one moved. Then, in a simultaneous uproar of pent-up emotion and outrage, the crowd rose up out of their chairs and charged the front table. A few unlucky players slipped on the numbered balls and leaned against others in a vain attempt to stay upright. It was a free-for-all of shouts and flailing arms and legs.

Several players eyed Elbow with suspicion. One shouted, "That guy's pickin' the balls. It's rigged!"

Elbow knew when to beat a hasty retreat. It really wasn't his fault, but he wasn't going to stay around to argue the point. He scooted out the back kitchen door, closing it firmly behind him. That should keep them busy for the moment.

He looked around. The truck was gone! Wilma's sons left sometime during the game and he didn't notice. He looked down the access road.

Luckily, the overloaded truck was slow to get up to speed. The truck's red taillights were still visible in the distance.

He heard pounding from behind the closed kitchen door. Time for plan B, whatever that was. He scanned the immediate area. The golf cart was just sitting there behind the office. No telling how much power was left on the battery, but anything to get away right now was better than nothing. He jumped in and put it in gear just as the kitchen door burst open. The crowd of angry bingo bashers came spilling out.

"He's making a run for it!"

"Get him!"

"Everyone get your trikes. He's getting away."

The crowd hurried to their tricycles parked in front of the bingo hall. Twenty of them set out in a frenzied posse, careening down the dark access road in hot pursuit at a mighty three miles per hour.

Elbow poured on as much power as the second-hand golf cart could stand. Behind him he could see the jiggling, white headlights of the three-wheelers as they pushed toward him on the gravel road. Up ahead he could see the red tail lights of the truck.

"Come on, baby," he urged the old cart. "I don't relish being beaten up by a group of angry, retired, bingo players on tricycles."

Elbow was gaining on the lethargic truck. He leaned on the cart's horn to attract the attention of the driver. The truck slowed. It stopped in the middle of the road just as Elbow turned his head around to check on the tricycles. He looked up just in time to steer the cart sharply to the right to prevent a collision and avoid imprinting the truck license plate permanently on his forehead. The cart sailed off the edge of the road at full speed and landed thirty feet into the swamp, upside down in the dark tangle of brush and murky water.

CHAPTER 21: TICKET TO RIDE

Wilma's sons got out of the truck to see what was happening. They saw the overturned cart from the road but didn't dare venture into the swamp to attempt a rescue. The army of angry tricycle riders arrived at the scene and focused their dim headlights on the slowly sinking golf cart.

"You think he's still under there?" Someone asked. "Maybe someone should go in there to make sure."

"No, he's a goner. There's gators in there."

"Serve him right messing up the bingo game like that."

"Maybe we should call someone. Anybody got a cell phone?"

The truck driver retrieved his phone and called 911. Within a few minutes sirens were heard approaching. Two fire trucks and a squad car barreled down the narrow road, lights flashing and horns blaring. The police rapidly took control of the situation and shifted the Leisure Paradise citizens backward and the moving truck forward, out of the way, so the firefighters could work.

Even though it was an electric cart, the firefighters doused it with retardant foam to prevent a fire. It was overkill, considering the situation, but it was a slow night at the fire station, and they were bored with reruns. One of them waded into the swamp and attached heavy chains to the cart bumper. A hoist on the front of one of the fire trucks made short work of dragging the cart up onto the road. No sign of Elbow.

"We'll have to wait till morning to search the swamp," the fire captain told them. "I won't risk sending my men in there until daylight. The gators are almost invisible at night. If that Elbow fellow is in there, the gators may find him before we do."

A noticeable wave of disappointment passed through the retirement crowd. The thought of alligators getting Elbow before they did dashed their hope of retaliation for the bingo fiasco.

Out of sight and away from the fire truck search lights, a lone figure crawled up the gravel embankment, covered in fire-retardant foam and swamp goo, and clung to a front tire of the rental truck.

On impact, somehow Elbow got tossed through the front of the cart but struggled free of the water, scrub trees, and underbrush in the darkness. Instinct told him to lie low. He'd made it to the truck. Somehow he had to get *on* the truck. It was his ticket to freedom.

He stood slowly to assess the situation and heard angry grumbles from the tricycle crowd. He needed to hide inside the truck where no one could see him. The front cab was small and cramped, only big enough for two passengers, so that was out. The back was crammed to the gills with Wilma Foley's monstrous theater organ and ornate Victorian furniture. Even if he could get the rear door open without anyone seeing him, there was no room to hide in there. Hiding on the truck undercarriage on that gravel road was asking for disaster.

Well, there was always the top. He had done it before under, shall we say, similar circumstances. Carefully, he climbed the front bumper and slid onto the left fender, flatting himself like a ninja. So far so good. Once on the hood, he crawled onto the cab roof, being careful not the drip any foam or swamp water on the windshield where it would be noticed. From there he lifted himself onto the roof of the cargo bay deflating himself as low as possible. If he was lucky and no one looked up, he would be invisible in the dark while all the lights and everyone's attention was focused on the ground and in the swamp.

Then he saw his shoes. That damn slivery, aluminum paint. They glowed like spotlights on his feet. Staying perfectly flat against the truck roof, he slowly, carefully bent one knee and brought the offending shoe close to his hand and slipped it off his foot. Then, just as carefully, he bent his other knee and removed the other one. He tucked the shoes in his shirt to hide the gleam and breathed a sigh of relief.

Elbow watched as the police took statements and told everyone to go on their way. The Foley boys got in the truck and started it up. The whole thing shook as the abused, rental motor warmed up. Elbow held tightly onto the front edge of the roof to prevent being vibrated over the side. A rough grinding of the gears and they were off with a jerk. Elbow looked back at the fire trucks and police car, but no one gave the truck a second glance.

Homeless again. He'd left all his clothes behind. He smelled like rotten swamp water. Twenty people were after him for breaking up a bingo game. He was clinging to the top of a swaying rental truck in the middle of nowhere. He smiled. It was just like old times. Life was grand.

CHAPTER 22: BAR MAGNIFICO

Elbow was almost giddy with the thought of being free at last. Visions of beer and lying back down to sleep until noon danced in his head. He was surprised he hadn't thought about Marcie all week. Getting the heck out of paradise had consumed all his thinking time.

The truck bumped along into the night. Elbow reminded himself to pay attention and hang onto the top edge or risk slipping off and eating gravel or getting dumped in the swamp again.

Soon lights appeared ahead intersecting with the highway. At the first stoplight, Elbow figured they would turn right, pass the mall and maybe a bar or two. Bars meant beer and friendly bar patrons who might give him a more comfy ride back to familiar territory.

When the truck stopped at the light, Elbow sat up and put on his shoes. Traffic was light and no one was around to notice. When the light turned green, the truck chugged into gear and turned left. Where were they going? There was nothing but swamp for a hundred miles in that direction. Elbow almost shouted out that they were headed the wrong way.

The truck sluggishly built up to speed on the smooth highway. Wind whipped past at fifty miles per hour. Lightning flashed in the dark clouds ahead. Soon huge drops of rain began to hit the truck, pelting him with stinging force. The rain quickly drenched him, washing away the fire-retardant foam and most of the swamp goo.

The top of the truck was slippery. The slightest movement of the truck to one side or the other sloshed his body around. He stubbornly hung onto the edge and hoped the driver wouldn't make a quick stop and send him sliding onto the top of the cab or the hood.

Just when he resigned himself to a hundred miles of pure misery, the truck groaned through the gears and slowed. They turned into a small parking lot and stopped. The sign above the door of a small, ratty building said BAR MAGNIFICO in bright blue neon. Either the

Foley boys hadn't had enough beer during the afternoon of loading the truck or it was a pit stop. Elbow wasn't going to stay on the cab roof long enough to find out.

As soon as they were out of sight, he let himself down to the roof of the cab and then lowered his feet to the ground. Parts of his body complained about the rough toss into the swamp with the golf cart, but he had been through worse scrapes. His shirt sleeve was torn, but he wasn't bleeding anywhere, so he sucked it up and started for the door.

He noticed motorcycles clustered in the parking lot. This was a biker bar. That could be either a good thing or a bad thing. You never knew. And it was Friday night too—probably a little rough around the edges in there. Well, forewarned is forearmed.

A flash of lightning singed the clouds above him. Inside, the atmosphere was smoky, humid, and dark. Except for the brightly lit bar, he could barely see two feet in front of him. A few heads turned in his direction, but his torn shirt and bedraggled appearance somehow ID'd him as a kindred spirit. He moved toward the bar unchallenged. So far so good.

The girl behind the bar was a shapely brunette with a heart tattooed on her neck and a barbed wire design around one wrist. Elbow gave her one of his patented, friendly smiles and ordered a beer.

She gave him the once-over with her eyes. "I never seen you before, tiger. You're not from around here, are you?"

"Ah, no, just thirsty." He tried to keep it neutral. With a girl like that in a place like this, she was sure to be somebody's main squeeze. No sense getting beaten up for being too friendly. Still, she was mighty fine to look at. Mighty fine.

He paid for the beer, said thanks and moved off to find an empty perch where he could enjoy the beer and survey the room. The two Foley boys were off in a back corner chatting up some bikers wearing skull and crossbone bandanas. If he stayed low, they probably would pass by and not recognize him.

Elbow gave the action around the pool table his attention. Two groups of bikers, wearing different colors, were having a little grunt match. Some guy named Big Eddy was taking a ribbing from a tall, skinny dude named Slim. So far it was all friendly, but Big Eddy was putting back a lot of beer in the abundant belly that hung over his studded, biker belt. If Eddy lost his sense of humor to the beer, the mood in the room would change pretty quickly. Elbow measured the distance to the door with his eyes and opted for a safer vantage point.

The tattooed bar girl came around with a tray to collect the empties. She gave him another smile. "You look a little lost, honey. You got girl troubles?"

"No, not girl troubles, transportation troubles," he said.

"Your car break down?"

"Yeah, sort of. It ended up in the swamp." Elbow's method was always tell something with a grain of truth, then you never have to remember what you made up.

"Oh, that's a bummer," she said. "Where you headed?"

"Miami."

"Well, that's simple enough. I get off at two. I can give you a lift," she smiled.

"Mighty kind of you."

"You want another beer? Same kind?"

"Yeah, thanks." He smiled friendly like and put ten bucks on her tray.

She pivoted neatly and headed back to the bar. He bent down to pretend to tie one of his aluminum tennis shoes so no one would think anything of their conversation. You never knew who was watching. He smiled to himself and tried hard to keep his eyes on the pool game. Things were definitely looking up.

CHAPTER 23: BIKER BRAWL

As predicted, the pool game between Big Eddy and Slim became a grudge match. Both were a little blurry-eyed and careless, but Slim had the advantage.

When the final shot made Slim the winner, he slammed his pool cue down on the table. "Pay up, you big tub of lard. Two hundred bucks!"

Bar conversation stopped cold. A slow rumble drifted through the place as feet hit the floor and, like the Red Sea parting, the two biker gangs grouped into opposing sides, ready to defend the honor of their respective brotherhoods.

The only sound came from the jukebox twanging out a song of passion and regret as the rival gangs starred at one another. Jose, the owner, lifted his shotgun off the wall. "Take it outside," he said cycling the action.

Elbow moved out of the way, slowly inching his way to the door, trying to look invisible. He wasn't quite quick enough. A bolt of lightning, with a deafening sonic boom, hit the electric pole outside in the parking lot. The bar was plunged into total darkness. Fists swung. Chaos ensued.

Elbow grabbed the door handle and pushed. A sudden wave of heavy bodies rushed the opening, slamming him into the door as it swung open, and catapulting him into the side of the building.

The crowd spilling out into the parking lot was armed with knives and chains. The emergency spotlight on the roof flickered on, illuminating the motorcycle gladiators with an eerie orange glow. Heads were getting whacked, bikes knocked down. It was a free-for-all. A biker with attitude came at Elbow swinging a studded chain over his head. The biker zigged. Elbow zagged and ducked. The chain cracked another biker dude in the forehead behind him. The dude took exception to being whacked and flattened the attitude.

It was time to find some shelter. Elbow kept low and made his way to the safety of the truck. He was almost there when two beer-bellied bikers with knives rolled into him and pushed him up against the rear tire. One of them was trying to give the other another hole in his earlobe.

Elbow didn't want his earlobe pierced and squeezed out from under them and swam through wet gravel to safety under the truck. He rolled over and breathed a sigh of relief.

A pair of shapely legs in high heels appeared in on the dark side of the truck.

"You better get yourself out from under there," the bar maid said, "Those guys might want to move the truck."

Elbow crawled out, stood up next to her and brushed sticky gravel from his shirt.

"Sorry, those goons are always lookin' to beat somebody up. We didn't get properly introduced. I'm Ellie." She offered her hand.

It didn't exactly seem like the perfect time for formal introductions but he took her hand and shook it. "Pleased to meet you. I'm Elbow."

"Follow me," she whispered. She led him into the shadow on the side of the building and around the back. "My car's over there." She motioned to a hunk of dented metal. "It ain't too fancy, but it runs real good and nobody ever wants to steal it. You can't be too careful workin' in a joint like this."

Elbow tried to open the passenger door.

"Oh, that door don't open too good. You gotta climb in the window," she told him.

Elbow climbed in. Evidently the window didn't work either. The torn bucket seat was wet from the rain, but it didn't matter. He was still wet from the rain too. It was transportation. Anything was better than the top of the truck. Ellie started the engine and guided the car around the other side of the building. When they reached the front parking lot, she gunned it and rocketed up onto the highway, spraying gravel into the fighting mass.

A few miles down the highway, a couple squad cars passed them going full throttle with lights blazing and sirens blasting. Ellie giggled. "They're headed for the *Magnifico*. I hope they brought their guns and maybe a gallon of pepper spray. The boys were really riled up tonight."

"Is it like that all the time?"

"Most times. The storm got them all jittery like, but they buy more beer and drop a lot of tips then too. Makes em feel all masculine or somethin'. So where are we headed, Elbow?"

"Anywhere near Miami."

"You from there?" She asked.

"Ah, yeah, mostly. I lived a lot of places."

"Yeah, me too. But this is the only job I could get just now."

"I can't believe that. A beautiful lady like you? Why I know places that would fall all over themselves to hire you."

"Really? Like where?"

"Well, Key West, maybe. They got lots of places, bars and restaurants."

"Oh, I would love to work someplace fancy like Hooters or even Denny's."

"Sure, you'd be perfect."

She smiled at him. "Say, you look like you could use a little freshening up. My place is just beyond the beach in south Miami. Want to come and use the shower? I could even run and get us burgers."

"Sounds great." Elbow stretched back in the torn bucket seat and looked at Ellie. She was sweet but a little dumb. Yes sir, things were definitely looking up.

CHAPTER 24: ELLIE

Ellie's apartment was above an Asian grocery store a few blocks from the beach. The stairway smelled strongly of soy sauce and sour cabbage. The landing at the top of the stairs was illuminated by a single forty-watt bulb.

"The place isn't much, but I got it fixed up real nice," she said as she opened the door.

Elbow looked around at the single room. There was a double bed in one corner, a makeshift kitchen with a table in another, and a sort of bathroom behind a shower curtain near the door. The walls were painted bright yellow. The bedsheets were red and the window had purple drapes.

"Real nice," Elbow nodded. "Colorful."

"Yeah. It ain't real big but it makes me feel all happy and comfy to walk in here every day."

"Yeah, you're a comfy and colorful kind of girl."

"I'm gettin' hungry. You can use the shower and I'll go get us some burgers. You want em with ketchup or mustard?"

"Ketchup."

"Ketchup! Me too!"

Elbow handed her a twenty.

"Oh my, you are a gentleman. Enjoy the shower. I'll be right back." She buzzed out the door.

Elbow surveyed the rusty pipe dangling out of the ceiling and the curled-up linoleum on the floor with a drain cut in one corner. Where it drained to was anybody's guess, but he wasn't fussy. The warm water felt good and it was great to soap off the swamp goo and gravel.

His clothes were a bit odorous. The shower soap had a strong manly fragrance and helped disguise it. Manly soap. Maybe Ellie had a boyfriend after all. His jeans were still damp so he dried them with Ellie's hair dryer and they weren't too bad, at least wearable.

Ellie returned with the burgers. "You wouldn't believe how busy they were at the Burger Bonanza. You'd think they were givin' them away. I hope you don't mind but I got drinks and fries too. It's been so long since I splurged. I gotta watch my figure so I don't splurge too often. I'll just change into somethin' better than these leather shorts and vest they make me wear at work. You wouldn't believe the looks I got at the Burger Bonanza take out. They weren't a gentleman like you."

She smiled and disappeared into the bathroom. When she reemerged she was dressed in bright yellow shorts and a matching yellow blouse with ruffles decorating the cleavage. Elbow blinked at the bright glare of color. He observed how it fit her as tightly as the leather outfit but it seemed to make her relaxed and happy.

She spread out the bags of burgers and fries on the bed. "It'll be just like a picnic," she gushed.

Elbow bit into the burger. It was juicy with just the right amount of ketchup. "You have a boyfriend?" He asked. "I mean a pretty girl like you probably has to fight them off with a stick."

"Aren't you sweet. Yeah, sometimes, but it's real hard to date somebody. I work nights and most guys work days. My days and nights are all upside down and backwards like."

"You ever date anyone from the Magnifico?" he asked.

"Hell no. Those guys are idiots. All they care about is their bikes. Rumble, rumble. They don't treat a girl right, you know? You got a girlfriend?" she asked.

"Ah...yeah, used to, but she went up north to work at Disney."

"Oh, wouldn't it be wonderful to waltz around in those big, floaty skirts and wear a sparkly, little tiara like Cinderella or Snow White!" She closed her eyes and pretended to swish a skirt around with her arms. Elbow knew a good thing when he saw it.

She sighed. She smiled. He didn't have to do anything more than smile back. She was in a dream world. She was Cinderella and he was Prince Charming.

CHAPTER 25: ESCAPE ARTIST

Elbow jolted awake around four. It took him a moment to get his bearings in the dark. He was sure he'd heard a door slam. Ellie lay next to him, taking up most of the bed. It was her bed so she was used to occupying all of it. He heard it—heavy footsteps climbing the stairs.

He was suddenly very alert. "Ellie, wake up," he whispered and shook her shoulder. "Someone's coming up the stairs. Wake up!"

"Huh?" she mumbled. "What is it?"

"Someone is coming up the stairs. You have a boyfriend?"

She rolled over. "Yeah, but I ain't seen him in a couple weeks. He might be in jail. Last time he was in jail was cause he beat up his fiancée."

There was nothing worse than getting caught in a girl's bedroom by a dude who had both a fiancée *and* a girlfriend. The door handle turned and someone tried to push at the door.

"Hey, Ellie, open up. It's me, Rocky."

Ellie sat straight up. "It's him. It's my boyfriend," she hissed. "You gotta get out of here!"

Elbow was already scrounging the floor for his clothes.

Rocky sounded a little inebriated. "Ellie, wake up! Open the door!"

"Yeah, sure. Just a minute, hon. I gotta find the key." She turned to Elbow trying to stuff his feet into his shoes. "You got to get out! He's mean when he's drunk. Out the window. It's the only way."

Elbow limped to the window, still trying to put on one shoe. He looked out. No fire escape, not even a ledge to hang onto. "You sure he won't beat on you once he gets in here?"

"Hell no. I can handle him, but thanks for asking, hon." She gave him a kiss on the cheek. "Just go. Go!" she whispered.

Rocky pounded on the door. "Open up!"

Elbow quickly crawled through the open window and hung from the sill as far down as he could reach. The Asian grocery store awning beneath him was his only hope. He could hear Ellie open the door and Rocky stumble into the room. Elbow let go of the window sill and did a freefall onto the awning. It held up pretty good but he hadn't calculated for the slope. He slid down and toppled ass-first toward the sidewalk. A pile of empty vegetable crates broke his fall. He scrambled and quickly rolled back along the sidewalk, out of sight, under the awning.

He heard Rocky above him at the window. "What was that? You got someone in here with you?"

"No, hon. Ain't nobody here but me. Must be them dam cats." Ellie told him.

Elbow said, "*Meow.*"

"I'll get him!" Rocky roared.

"No, hon, you just put that gun away! You can't see nothin' in the dark anyway. You shoot that thing off and somebody would call the cops for sure. A cat ain't worth another trip to jail."

Elbow couldn't hear any more. They must have moved away from the window. He stayed where he was under the awning until he was sure it was safe to move. One last peek at the window to be certain and he was off, sticking to the shadows.

He wasn't familiar with this part of Miami. There were shops on some of the streets and what looked like houses on the side streets with high walls and gates in front to keep out the riffraff or maybe drug lords lived there. It was hard to tell. Places like that had state of the art security systems or even their own armed entourage. Better keep moving.

The trick to moving through ritzy neighborhoods was to look like you belonged there and had someplace to go and you were going there. Of course it helped if it wasn't four in the morning and your shirt wasn't ripped and you weren't wearing aluminum painted tennis shoes, but attitude counted for a lot.

Several more blocks and he realized he was tired. He and Ellie didn't exactly get to sleep early and her boyfriend arrived at four. Nice kid, Ellie, but boyfriends with guns win every time. No sense getting mixed up with that. Thank goodness there was a window. He laughed. "Meow!" Maybe he had a new nickname, Elbow "the Cat."

He passed a side street and glimpsed a sliver of water at the end. Time for a little detour. Maybe there was a beach. Beaches were comfy places to sleep if you could find a little shelter under something to keep yourself hidden. At the end of the street was a NO TRESPASSSING sign. Signs like PRIVATE and KEEP OFF always made him itch to walk over, look and touch.

He surveyed the sand. There were shrubs up against a stone wall near the edge of someone's precisely manicured lawn. Perfect. Crawl under there and presto, comfy and protected. He looked around. The coast was clear. He found an opening under the shrubs and wiggled in under the low branches. It was a little damp, but the rain had quit and the air was still warm. He dug out a shallow hole to make his hips more comfy, curled up, and went to sleep.

CHAPTER 26: DOGFIGHT

The buzz of a fly landing on his nose woke him up. A small green lizard raced across his face to catch the tasty morsel for breakfast, then scurried away up into the branches of the shrub above him. Nothing like sleeping rough to get you back in touch with nature. Elbow blinked his eyes a few times to get in focus. He could hear waves and a boat motor. The warmth of filtered sunlight on his back felt good.

He stretched his legs. He was stiff. Oh yeah, the bar fight and the crash landing on the sidewalk. There would be bruises, of course, but no knife wounds or bullets holes this time. He rolled over and peeked out at the beach. What time was it? The sun was already hard at work roasting the sand.

He was just about to crawl out of his hiding place when a solitary figure walked through the gate in the stone wall and headed for the edge of the water to test it with her toe. She wore a huge sunhat and arranged a striped beach towel neatly on the sand before removing her robe and sunglasses and placing them in a large straw carry bag. Oh my, she was fine in a striped bikini that matched the towel. Elbow stayed hidden and enjoyed the view.

She strolled into the water up to her thighs, then reached up to coil her long dark hair on top of her head. Waves gently caressed her body as she slowly entered the sea. Fine, mighty fine.

If not for the dog, Elbow would have stayed in his comfortable hiding place, admiring the view. The beast was a shaggy mutt of miscellaneous parentage with a bad attitude and lots of teeth. It came roaring out of the street and rushed toward the water's edge, barking and snarling at the woman in the water.

"Help!" she cried. "Help! It's that maniac dog again. Miguel! Where the hell are you, Miguel? Get him out of here!"

The dog trotted into the water up to its belly and growled. Elbow rolled out from under the hedge and sprinted toward the water. On the way, he grabbed the towel off the sand and wrapped it around his fist like he once saw a guy do in a movie. The dog turned and gave Elbow a snarl, then lunged. Elbow stuck out his towel-wrapped hand. The dog took the bait and clamped its jaws on the wad of towel. In one move, Elbow swung his arm around in a circle about four feet off the ground, with the dog firmly attached.

Now what? Maybe it wasn't such a great idea after all. He couldn't keep twirling around in circles forever. The dog got bored going around like a tilt-a-whirl before Elbow did and let go. It sailed twenty feet up the beach before landing teeth over tail in the sand. A little dizzy and unsteady, but not deterred from its mission of chewing someone up, it staggered back toward Elbow.

The dog wasn't taking the hint. Time for firmer measures. The dog came at him, but all Elbow had to defend himself with was sand. At least there was plenty of that. He bent over and started scooping sand in a great whirlwind, throwing and whipping it at the hound.

The dog stopped, not sure what to do. It complained about sand in its mouth and eyes. It shook himself vigorously to ward off the onslaught of stinging sand. Elbow poured it on even more.

The woman in the bikini emerged from the sea and took a cell phone from the large straw bag. "Where the hell are you?! I've got World War Three going on down here on the beach with some guy and Mr. Crazy's damned dog. Get down here and shoot something!"

Elbow used a moment when the dog was confused to wrap the towel around the dog's neck and pull him up in a sort of choke hold. The mutt didn't exactly have a neck and quickly twisted free. Elbow grabbed the large, straw bag, dumped the contents onto the sand and met the charging dog head on to scoop it up in the bag. The dog immediately tried digging its way out.

"You got all my stuff full of sand!" The woman shouted.

Elbow thought she obviously didn't fully comprehend the seriousness of the situation. "Give me a hand here, will you! This dog will chew his way out in no time."

"What am I supposed to do, say 'bad dog' and he'll just stop?"

"Well do SOMETHING or he'll have both of us for breakfast!"

Just then the cavalry arrived in the form of a rather large man in a suit with a gun. "Who you want me to kill? This guy?" he gestured at Elbow.

"No, the dog, stupid. It came after me again. This guy's been keeping it busy until you finally got here."

The dog's head popped out of the top of the bag. Evidently it had prior altercations with the muscle suit and one sniff of the guy's strong aftershave was enough to make it change course and try to chew through the other side of the bag with sudden urgency.

Elbow loosened his grip on the bag and the dog was out and halfway across the sand toward the street before the suit could pull off more than one shot.

"Did you get it?" she asked.

"Nah, it was too quick. Or maybe this jerk let it loose on purpose."

"Don't be dense. This guy, whoever he is, kept that hell hound off of me. Help me find my earrings. They got dumped out in the sand. My phone's a mess too. And I'll need a new bag. This one's got dog slobber all over it." She left everything there in the sand and walked off toward the gate to the lawn. "Bring the dog guy up to the house, Miguel, the damn dog tore his shirt. Maybe we can find him a new one."

Miguel was obviously protection muscle. Elbow wasn't going to ask who or what he was protecting. The guy motioned Elbow with his gun to follow the bikini up the walkway to the house.

CHAPTER 27: HOSPITALITY

Elbow approached the house with curious caution, trying to look casual, while the muscle guy behind him watched to make sure he didn't touch the grass. The house was unnecessarily big with a lot of fake carved Italian stuff and cupids around the doors and windows.

Elbow inspected the veranda and spotted more muscle behind a potted fig tree. Whoever owned the place liked to keep this slice of paradise free from intruders. The muscle suit motioned for him to go around to the side entrance. Evidently the veranda entrance was for invited guests, not dog wrestlers. He didn't mind. If it was the kitchen, there might be food for breakfast instead of lizards and sand.

Mr. Muscle punched numbers into the keypad and grunted. Elbow assumed that meant he was to enter. The door was a double-thick, steel beauty that wouldn't have looked out of place in a prison movie. They walked down a long, windowless hallway and turned right, into a brightly lit kitchen. Two ladies in aprons, one older, one younger, immediately jumped to attention.

"You hungry?" the muscle suit asked.

"Ah yeah, I could eat," Elbow told him.

The suit looked Elbow's slender frame up and down, laughed and said, "Yeah, you look like you could use a few doughnuts. Fix him up, Concetta. I'll be right back."

Concetta did just as she was told and didn't ask any questions. She got busy with a couple of slices of coffee cake, orange juice and coffee. The younger woman smiled shyly and pointed at Elbow's aluminum tennis shoes. His Spanish was a little rusty but he was sure Concetta told her to shut up in Spanish.

Elbow plowed through the coffee cake, juice, and coffee. The coffee cake was perfection with a crunchy topping of cinnamon and sugar. The juice was freshly squeezed, and the coffee was obviously a private blend that Starbucks could never afford to sell. Whoever these people were, they lived like royalty with their fake Italian villa, good food, steel doors, private beach and armed protection. The bikini was maybe expensive eye candy. It all screamed drug lord or maybe exiled Latin dictator. The sooner he thanked everyone for their hospitality and got the hell out the better.

The muscle suit returned carrying a black shirt on a hanger. The woman from the beach followed him into the kitchen.

"Miguel, make him take off that ripped, plaid shirt and put this one on," she ordered.

Miguel made a motion with his thumb for Elbow to stand and try on the shirt. It didn't seem like a good time to argue so he unbuttoned his shirt and took it off.

The woman gasped. The golf cart dive into the swamp, the bar fight and the awning caper bruises were beginning to bloom brilliant purple on his chest and back. She reached out her hand to touch them. Elbow backed away a couple of inches.

"The dog did that to you?" she asked.

"No. No, these are from last night. I did a little escape thing and had a bit of an altercation with a couple of bikers. Nothing serious."

"Does it hurt?"

"I've had worse."

"Your face looks fine."

"I know how to duck. The other guys had knives."

The woman and the muscle suit exchanged a look. The woman shifted onto one hip. "You certainly knew what to do with that miserable dog."

"Sorry about the towel and the straw bag, but it was better than getting bit," Elbow said.

"Try on the shirt," she said.

Elbow slipped it onto his arms and buttoned a few buttons. It fit like a glove. She nodded approval, took his torn shirt and dropped it on the floor in front of Concetta. Concetta must have been used to being treated like a human waste basket. She picked it up gingerly with two fingers and deposited it in a garbage can.

The woman looked Elbow up and down. "Where are you from?" She asked.

"Around. Miami sometimes. Key West. A few places. I'm sort of between jobs at the moment."

The woman gave him another look, turned rapidly on her heel and walked out.

"Thank the lady for the shirt, will you?" Elbow told the muscle suit. "It's real nice."

The suit grunted. "Just curious, but where did you mix it up with the bikers?"

"A place out on the swamp road, the Magnifico. Some guy wasn't too keen to pay his pool bet and there were insults and then the place sort of blew up and rolled out into the parking lot."

"Yeah, I heard about that. And you walked away?"

"Well, I was kind of keen to not get holes in my torso. I didn't want to get any blood, mine or anyone else's, on my nice, plaid shirt."

The guy chuckled then turned serious. "What were you doin' on the beach this morning?" he asked.

Elbow smiled to give himself a few seconds to think up a good cover story instead of confessing he slept under the hedge. "I was walking along the avenue and saw the ocean at the end of the street. I thought I'd take a look. Then I saw the dog and just tried to keep it off of the lady. I didn't mean to trespass."

The guy gave him a hard look, nodded his head and left the room. Elbow observed they certainly came and went kind of fast around there. He buttoned the rest of the shirt and tucked it in his jeans. It was a great shirt, maybe even silk. The muscle guy had one too, along with a matching black silk tie and a dark suit. It all looked great but must be hell to stand out in the sun in it.

The younger kitchen girl looked at him in the shirt and gave him a friendly smile. Concetta gave her an order. "Cici, clear away the empty breakfast things." Cici was quick to obey. Elbow tried giving Concetta a smile too, but she wasn't having any of it.

91

CHAPTER 28: JOB OFFER

E lbow tried out his rusty Spanish. *"El baño?"* He hoped it was the right word for bathroom.

Concetta gave him another stony gaze and pointed to the door to the hallway. Cici hurried to the door to show him the way, but Concetta turned her laser-gaze in her direction and the girl stopped in her tracks. Elbow wondered whether Concetta could burn holes in walls with her eyes too. He thanked her in Spanish and headed for the hallway.

There were five or six doors leading off in various directions from the hallway. He wasn't as much interested in finding the *el baño* as he was in the steel exit door at the end of the hallway. It was locked on the inside with another keypad. What kind of a place locks doors from both sides like that? The muscle suit appeared at the other end of the hallway with a panicked expression.

Elbow thought fast. "Ah, is this the bathroom?" He tried to look innocent.

The guy's face showed relief. He pointed to the door next to him. Evidently, extraneous people were not supposed to go wandering around looking for bathrooms or anything else.

"Thanks," Elbow said. He hoped the guy wouldn't try to accompany him into the bathroom just to keep tabs on him. Some things are private.

The bathroom was an inside room with no windows. Chances of escape from there were zero. Elbow used the opportunity to do a quick washup and get some sand out of his shoes and underwear. When he exited the bathroom, the muscle suit was still on guard in the hallway.

Elbow gave him a friendly smile. "Thanks, that feels better. My briefs were beginning to itch from all the sand."

"You're wanted upstairs," the guy told him. "Don't go wandering off like that again or someone might use you for target practice, okay?"

"Sure, I got it. But why all the heavy stuff? What is this place anyway?"

The guy just motioned for him to walk back through the kitchen and up the narrow stairs to the second floor. After a few twists and turns Elbow lost track of where he was. He began to wish he had saved some sand to leave a trail to find his way back.

They entered a hallway lined with plush carpets and gold-trimmed mirrors. At the end was a set of tall, carved doors. The muscle suit motioned for Elbow to stop, then knocked gently on one door. The door opened and another muscle suit looked them up and down and allowed them to enter.

A small older man behind an ornately carved desk looked up and motioned Elbow to come forward. The second muscle guy gave him a nudge. Elbow walked. The older man came around the front of the desk to look him over. He had dark hair and a dark mustache that curved downward around his mouth. His suit was impeccably tailored for his small frame, but his eyes were mean and cold.

"So you're the fellow who saved Anita from the dog."

"Ah, yes sir," Elbow said, not sure where this was going.

"You frisked him, Miguel?"

"Yeah, he ain't got nothin' on him."

"That was pretty brave of you. That mutt should be put down or have all its teeth extracted." The man laughed and the two suits laughed in unison. The man looked Elbow up and down again with his cold eyes. "You got guts. I like guys with guts. The way Anita tells it, you think pretty fast on your feet too. I like guys who jump in to do what it takes, you know?" The way the man said it made the hair on the back of his neck stand up.

Elbow smiled slightly, not sure how to react.

"Yeah, I got to take care of her. She's...a friend. A bit headstrong maybe but I take care of her real good. I wouldn't like it if she got bite marks on her from a damn mutt. Miguel says maybe you're looking for work. Maybe I give you a job makin' sure she doesn't get bite marks on her. What do you think?"

"Ah, I don't know. I was just passing through on my way to a friend's place in Miami."

The man gave Elbow a pat on the shoulder. "It's all settled then. You come work for me. You go with her shopping, the hair dresser, the beach, everywhere. You make sure she doesn't get bit, yes? Miguel, you fix him up with some clothes. He can't go with her looking like that."

Miguel nodded. The man went back to his desk and waved his hand. They were dismissed. Miguel grabbed Elbow's arm and steered him back out to the hallway.

Elbow wiggled his arm loose and turned around to face the muscle suit. "Look, I don't mean to be rude or anything, but this is getting pretty strange. Nobody tells me anything. You don't even know my name, and I don't have a clue who you are or where I am or what he thinks I'm supposed to do."

The guy put his finger to his lips to indicate silence and motioned with his thumb to move on down the hall. They came to a door at the end like all the others, but this one had a keypad like the back door. The suit punched in some numbers and the door opened.

CHAPTER 29: PROTECTION

The room was bare, lined along one wall with pale green lockers. It was a stark contrast to the ornate hallway on the other side of the door.

The muscle suit finally spoke. "You're a pretty lucky dude. It isn't everyone the boss takes to right away. His girl, Miss Gonzales, must have put in a good word. I'm Miguel." He held out his hand.

Elbow shook it. The guy had quite a grip. "I'm Elbow. Look, all I did was stop a semi-rabid dog from chewing up a pretty lady. I'm not sure I want a job of official dog wrestler and girlfriend babysitter. Who is 'the boss' anyway and why does he need people with guns and a place built like Fort Knox?"

Miguel's face went stone cold. "Better you don't know. Let's just say he's a certain business man who doesn't like to be crossed. Just do your job and shut up, Elbow. That way there won't be any trouble. By the way, if it helps, the pay is pretty good."

"Yeah, but do you live long enough to spend it?"

Miguel ignored the last remark and opened the last locker in the row. It was hung floor to ceiling with black shirts, slacks, ties and jackets. He selected a few and handed them to Elbow. "Here, you better try these on. Miss Gonzales likes smart dressers."

Elbow tried on the slacks. He didn't have the bulging muscles of the muscle guys. The slacks were loose, especially around the waist. Miguel laughed and selected a black belt to match from the rack on the door. Miguel laughed some more when Elbow tried on the jacket. It hung on his shoulders like a small tent.

"Maybe I'll start a new fashion trend and just skip the jacket and tie," Elbow said.

Miguel grunted and got out a key to unlock another locker door. The interior made Elbow's eyes pop. It was lined with guns. Miguel selected one and handed it to Elbow.

"No thanks, I'm allergic to guns," Elbow explained.

"You might need it."

"I hate 'em. If this is a job where guns are necessary, I'm out. No thanks. If a person has a gun, someone else with a gun is likely to shoot at them and then where will you be, somewhere with holes in you. I'm pretty good at talking my way out of things and I know a hundred different ways to hide if things get dicey." He started taking off the slacks.

"Whoa, Anita—Miss Gonzales—is...how shall I say this? A little headstrong, like the boss says. She likes things her way, and sometimes people get a little...upset. You know what I mean?"

"And you need to fight them off with a gun?"

"Hell no, it's mostly for show unless it gets really necessary. The boss doesn't like things to get necessary. Then it gets *messy*. Let's just say he's not happy to attract attention and deal with the police in any way."

"What does he do anyway?"

Miguel's stony look returned. "Business. That's all you need to know. Your job is to make Anita safe and happy. And that doesn't include getting cozy. The boss wouldn't like it." He looked at Elbow's aluminum shoes. "But you're not her type. She likes 'em rich. I'll find you some dark shoes so you don't twinkle in the dark. You get a small room upstairs like the rest of us, some cash in case Miss Gonzales wants something special, three squares a day, free laundry, evenings and Thursdays off. Any questions?"

"Yeah, but I'm a little hazed over with everything so far, I don't know what to ask."

"She's got a schedule. I'll give it to you. When you're in or near the house you stay close but sort of out of sight. You don't want to hear any conversations but maybe stay close so she knows where you are. Outside the gate you stay close, like next to her or behind, so you got a good view of what's going on."

"You've done this before."

"Yeah, I was on Anita patrol once, but...now I got other things to do. You sure you don't want the gun?"

"No thanks, I'll see how it goes."

Miguel shrugged, put it back in the closet and locked it up. "Come on, I'll show you around."

From the furnished, residential rooms for staff on the top floor that had a panoramic view of a neighboring roof, to the exercise room in the basement and three sets of hidden stairways, it was quite a tour. When they entered the garage, Elbow marveled at the fine selection of cars.

"That's Miss Gonzales' car over there," Miguel said, pointing to the red Maserati. "You drive stick?"

"Ah, yeah, but it's been a while."

"That's okay. She usually drives, but sometimes she just stops in the middle of the street, gets out to shop and throws you the keys to park it. She gets tired of cars pretty fast and gets a new one a couple times a year."

"Yeah, they're a bore when they get dirty."

Miguel put on a half smile. "A word to the wise, Elbow, you can say stuff like that to me, but hold it back with her or the boss or you might get tossed out in the street pretty fast missing some teeth in the process."

"Thanks for the warning." Elbow frowned. He wasn't used to watching his mouth.

"Yeah, sure. Come on, I'll get you fixed up with a phone."

t

Elbow liked his new black shoes. They weren't the usual second-hand beauties he got at Good Will or Salvation Army that came with someone else's dented insoles. These fit just right, had clean insides and rubber soles for fast traction. His room came with all the comforts—TV, small fridge, shampoo, and even a toothbrush. The fact that it also came with guns was a little troubling, but he didn't have any place else to sleep except the beach so he settled in and tried to memorize where the exit stairs were.

The phone on his hip went off just as he was tuning in to Jerry Springer on his room TV. Miss Gonzales was anxious to shop. Elbow found the right staircase and joined her in the garage.

"Well, that took you a while," she said.

"Sorry, I'm new here. This place has more stairs than the funhouse in Atlantic City."

She pointed to the car. "Get in. I want to shop."

Elbow held the driver's side door for her and got into the passenger seat. She revved the engine a couple of times just for the hell of it while the garage door opened. Elbow reached for his seatbelt.

She laughed at him. "Don't worry, sweetie, I only rolled it once." She roared out of the garage into the alley. "By the way, what's your name?"

"Elbow," he said, trying to keep from grabbing the dashboard and screaming like a little girl as she did a full speed S-maneuver to avoid a dump truck.

"Elbow! Is that like a nickname or something? I see they got you some decent clothes. You look better." She shot out of the alley onto the main street without too much attention to details such as pedestrians or cars. "So, what's your story, cowboy? I don't see a gun. All the other guys got guns. You know karate or something?"

Elbow shrugged and did a fast grab at the arm rest as she ran the car around a corner. "I don't like guns. Besides, there's nowhere to hide it in this outfit. You're not expecting any trouble are you?"

"You never know. Didn't they give you a jacket and a tie?"

"The jacket fit like a circus tent. I'm not a real formal tie kind of guy."

She gave him a smile and was a little impatient with the speed limit. "What did you do before this?"

"Cleaned up coconuts in a leisure village."

"You're joking."

"Nope. Riding in a flash car with a well-dressed lady is a walk in the park compared to coconuts."

She giggled. "You're cute. Those other goons who work for Carlo are no fun. They don't talk to me. They think there are bad guys around every corner."

"Are there bad guys around every corner?"

"No, silly. For Carlo maybe, but not for me. Who'd want to mess with me?"

"Well, someone who wants to get at him through you maybe. You aren't exactly invisible with a fancy red car and posh clothes."

She pouted. "I don't like it when people talk to me like that!"

"Sorry. You asked, so I told you. I'll just shut up, hang on and look for bad guys."

She came to a screeching halt and pulled diagonally into a parallel parking spot. "A parking place right in front of the store! You must be good luck."

"You mind if I re-park a little and get the rear end of the car out of the street? Parking tickets are such a nuisance."

"Yeah, sure." She glanced at her closed door, then at Elbow. "Well?"

Elbow got out of the car and walked around to open her car door for her. Her skirt was short and her legs were long as she exited the car. Elbow admired with his eyes.

"You like what you see?" She tossed him the keys.

"Very nice," he said, deliberately looking at the car. She smiled. She knew they weren't talking about the car.

He escorted her to the door to the lingerie store and held that open for her too. He returned to the car and slid into the low, soft leather, driver's seat. Everything about it, even the smell, said money. He started the engine. It was a powerful engine. For a moment he daydreamed what it must be like to change cars a couple of times a year. Maybe the way the lady drove, it was a necessity. He came out of his mental fantasyland and re-parked the car so it didn't obstruct traffic. He got out and walked toward the store entrance, keeping an eye out for invisible bad guys.

CHAPTER 31: OVERLOAD

As soon as Elbow opened the lingerie shop door and stepped inside, a floral overload attacked his senses. This place was a private women's world of pink walls and crystal chandeliers where men shouldn't venture except when forced to for Valentine's day or Christmas. The place was so feminine it gave him the jitters.

Miss Gonzales was busy inspecting a table of little lace things in a rainbow of colors. She held up two small, lace panties, one red, the other bright green. "Which do you think?" she asked.

Elbow took a deep breath. "Red," he said.

"Yeah, red. The green looks like puke. She waved the pair around. "Women wear red in Italy on New Year's for good luck."

Elbow smiled politely. It was more information than he wanted to know.

She lassoed a salesgirl. "You got a bra to match?" She asked.

Elbow wasn't going there. He quickly found the comfy chair where husbands and significant others wait the interminable wait for the fairer sex to decide between red, pink, blue, or puke. Frankly, guys weren't too picky about the color of a girl's underwear, just whether it had too many hooks or snaps.

Elbow did a fast look around for any nasty characters like he was supposed to, but the two sales girls were no threat. If this was what this job was going to be like, a wild ride against traffic one minute and mind numbing waiting the next, he wasn't sure he could stick it. He sat back and suddenly thought of hauling coconuts and realized almost anything was better than coconuts.

He needed something to help him wait. He imagined what Miss Gonzales might look like in the red panties and bra. It made him smile but maybe imagining it wasn't a good idea. The boss might not like it. He turned to imagining the skinny salesgirl in the green set. That was amusing but not nearly as stimulating.

Miss Gonzales finished her selection and checked out. As she walked to the door she handed Elbow the little pink bag to carry for her. It must have weighed all of six ounces but she didn't want to be burdened.

"I need some shoes," she announced and headed for the ritzy store down the block.

Elbow followed, scanning the sidewalk for small, venomous dogs or guys who might be hiding guns under their jackets. No men or dogs anywhere, just women of all ages dressed to the nines, out power-shopping for more posh duds. He wondered whether it was a hobby, or whether they were training for a new Olympic sport.

Anita stopped in front of the door to the shoe store. Elbow jumped to open the door before she got impatient waiting and might have to actually open it herself. Inside, shoes lined the clear glass shelves floor to ceiling, illuminated by miniature spotlights. It certainly was a far cry from the bargain sneaker table at Goodwill.

She strolled along the display, inspecting the five-inch heels with sequins. Elbow tried to keep his mind elsewhere, but the sight of her hips, in that short skirt, slowly walking along was mesmerizing. He almost had to slap himself to get his mind back to business.

A sales clerk approached. He was dressed in a tight, black jacket, skinny pants and white ruffles cascading down the front of his shirt. Miss Gonzales obviously knew him. They exchanged air kisses and he admired her shoe selections. Elbow kept an eye on him, but the guy was only looking for a big sale and was no threat except to her pocket book.

After forty-five minutes trying on thirty pairs of shoes, she was finally ready. She bought three pairs of shoes, all with sequins, because she couldn't decide which pair she liked best. Elbow thought maybe she should try a little aluminum paint if she really wanted glitz. It would save a bundle for her next Maserati.

She left the shopping bag with the shoes on the counter for Elbow to carry. He was beginning to get the hang of the shopping thing. He was the bodyguard/carry-all guy. It still beat coconuts but he didn't feel useful, just used. He held the door for her again and they exited the store.

She suddenly stopped in the middle of the sidewalk and announced, "I'm hungry. Let's go to Buster Burger. I just love their fries." She turned and headed back to the car. "Keys," she said, and held out her hand. Elbow rummaged in his pocket, produced the keys and managed to open the car door for her one-handed. She popped the trunk. He deposited the shopping bags in the back, then strapped himself into the passenger seat. He said a small prayer as she revved the engine and touch-bumped the BMW in front of them and the Roller behind several times to move out of the parking spot.

Bumpers and gleaming finishes still intact, she zipped down the street several blocks and did a sharp left into a less fashionable part of town.

CHAPTER 32: BUSTER BURGERS

The Buster Burger was a greasy little dive in the middle of a neighborhood where every house seemed to have a derelict car or two in the front yard. By contrast, the Maserati was a little conspicuous. She parked it sideways in the parking lot, taking up several parking places.

Elbow remembered his door duties and opened the car door for her. "You sure this place is okay?"

"Yeah, I eat here sometimes. Their fries are to die for."

It was just an expression, but Elbow gave the place a worried look and wondered if her choice of words was too close to the truth. Everything about it said rough and tough. It was a place he, himself, might frequent if he was alone, but his job was supposed to be keeping the lady safe. He tried not to be paranoid, but the place had TROUBLE written in big, invisible letters above the door.

It took Elbow's eyes a few seconds to adjust to the dark inside after entering from the bright parking lot outside. The interior did nothing to calm his fears. The walls hadn't seen a fresh coat of paint since the eighties. The counter and kitchen in back probably hadn't been cleaned since then either.

A couple of guys, who looked like they worked in construction, maybe concrete, lounged in the last, faded green booth along the front wall. They stopped talking and looked up as Miss Gonzales sashayed up to the counter. An old woman with frizzled gray hair and missing teeth turned her attention away from the TV set to take their order.

"You want a burger and fries too?" Miss Gonzales asked Elbow.

"Yeah. Well done, please." He figured if it was well done most of the crap might get burned off.

She left the counter and went to sit in one of the booths, leaving Elbow to pay for the order. Maybe they didn't take American Express Platinum. He paid with the extra cash Miguel had given him.

Just as he turned to join her in the booth, one of the construction guys got up from his seat, removed his hard hat and smoothed back his hair. The fellow's eyes were fixed on Miss Gonzales as he walked the length of the dented linoleum floor toward her booth. Oh hell. He was going to talk to her.

Elbow got there first and squeezed into the opposite seat. "Hi, there," he said friendly like.

The guy looked annoyed, but he smiled, revealing a nasty set of stained teeth. "I was goin' to talk to the lady," he said.

"Sure, talk away," Elbow told him. She turned to look out the fly-specked window.

"Alone," the guy said as he drew himself up to his full six-foot height.

Damn. This was not going well. Play it casual and maybe he'll get the hint. "Nah, anything you want to say you can say in front of me. I don't mind."

"I said alone!"

Miss Gonzales gave the guy a look that would have dropped a charging rhino in its tracks, then turned her gaze on Elbow as if to say "Do something."

"Sorry, but I think the lady just wants to eat, not talk," Elbow said.

The guy made a grab for Elbow's shirt. Elbow saw that coming before the guy ever left his own booth and kicked out from under the table directly at the guy's left knee cap. Knees are not designed to bend backwards. The guy folded in a groaning lump on the floor.

His buddy in the booth made a move to get up and get involved. Elbow turned toward him and just grinned ear to ear. The guy had second thoughts about messing with someone who was crazy and stayed where he was. Miss Gonzales looked at the big guy on the floor and then at slender Elbow in awe.

The old woman at the counter rang the service bell twice to signal their order was ready. *Ding ding!* End of round one!

Elbow got up from the table, stepped over the groaning man and went to collect the order. He brought the plastic baskets back to the table. "Let's get out of here and find a nice quiet park where we can eat in peace."

As they headed for the door, the old woman shouted at them, "Hey, you can't take them baskets outa here!"

"Better call an ambulance. The guy on the floor isn't going to walk out of here on his own," Elbow told her. The woman grunted. Maybe she was used to shoveling up bodies off the floor on a regular basis. He handed her a twenty for her trouble and she gave him a toothless grin.

They went to the car in the parking lot and Miss Gonzales tossed him the keys. "You drive."

Elbow climbed in the driver's seat and maneuvered the red sports car out of the parking lot. Sirens sounded in the distance. It was time they got back to more civilized territory.

CHAPTER 33: PICNIC IN THE PARK

Elbow drove a bit and kept an eye on the rear view mirror just in case the cops might be on the lookout for a red Maserati. He spotted a park with picnic tables and parked the car behind a large planting of shrubs so it was hidden from the street. There were kids playing baseball and a couple of skate boarders were scratching up the curbs around a small fountain. It seemed peaceful enough.

After attending to door-opening duties, they settled on a table under a tree. They tried the burgers, which were passable, and then the fries which were just as promised, crispy and delicious.

"Didn't you get any ketchup? I like mine with ketchup," Miss Gonzales complained and tried to look offended.

"I was a little busy keeping uninvited guests off the menu," he told her, "Unless you wanted to talk to the guy who looked like he ate tobacco for breakfast."

Elbow somehow didn't react the way she expected. She softened a little. "No. Where did you learn that kick thing? He fell over like a dead tree."

"Saw it in a movie."

"Miguel once had to pull a gun on a guy who was pushy and wanted to buy me a drink."

"I don't like guns. I kick, and in a tight squeeze I can bite too. There are quite a lot more places you can kick a guy than bite to make it hurt."

"You sound like you did this protection thing before."

"No, just protecting me. I seem to run into more than my share of...*situations*. Usually I don't stick around long enough to need to kick anything. I'm good at running down the sidewalk."

"You didn't run this time."

"If it was just me, yeah, but I couldn't leave you there at the mercy of Mr. Tobacco Breath."

"Thanks."

Elbow sensed it wasn't in her nature to say *thank you*, but she said it. "You're welcome." He winked.

She smiled. "What do I do if I'm like alone shopping?"

"Well, you have some powerful weapons on your feet right now. I'd hate to be on the receiving end of a kick with those things. They're pointed in front and back."

"These? But these are Prada's."

"Yeah, but whatever they are, they would leave a mark. Sometimes you got to choose between getting punched or doing the punching. I would hate to see you love your shoes so much you couldn't use them to protect yourself."

"I never thought about it like that."

She probably never thought about a lot of things, but he let it go. She wasn't the smartest woman he'd ever met but she sure was decorative.

She looked at him. "I can't figure you out."

"Oh yeah?"

She crossed her long legs and leaned on the picnic table. "I mean you're not like the rest of those guys who work for Carlo. You're different."

"Different?"

"Yeah, I can talk to you. Everyone else thinks I'm dense. They just do things for me because Carlo pays them. You actually tell me things."

"Maybe I'm not supposed to."

"No, I like it. You do cool stuff, like break knees. You can call me Anita." She gave him a smile. "You got a girlfriend?"

"A girlfriend? No, she went up to Orlando for a job."

Anita looked him up and down and smiled. Warning bells went off in Elbow's head. He could hear Miguel's voice: *The job doesn't include getting cozy, the boss wouldn't like it.*

Elbow scanned the surrounding shrubbery for prowling bad guys just to have something to do with his eyes. She was damned attractive and being flirty. Maybe he better change the subject as a diversion. "What about you and the boss? You been together long? He takes care of you real good."

"Carlo," she said and her face fell like a deflated balloon. "Yeah, he takes care of me, shoes and clothes and stuff, but he stays in the house all the time. He ever goes out. Sometimes I get so bored. I want to go out to clubs and dance someplace where I can show off my new shoes, you know?"

"Yeah, mighty pretty—the shoes I mean." He caught himself starting to get cozy. Time to collect the burger wrappers and napkins and get back to business. "You ready to go home or do you have more shopping to do?"

"It's kind of nice here," she said looking around at the trees and sky as if she just noticed them.

Elbow thought she probably didn't see much of the world around her except the inside of stores and an occasional dip in the ocean. "We can drive around the park if you want to see more," he said, "but you can't drive fast or it will all be a blur."

"You drive so I can look."

Elbow deposited their trash in the waste can near the parking lot and escorted her to the car. He took the wheel and they did a slow drive through the small park.

She laid her head back and took it all in. She suddenly sat straight up. "You know what I really want to do? I want to go to a movie. Carlo never takes me to a movie. Take me to a movie."

It was more a command than a request. He wasn't sure being alone with her in a dark movie theater was the best thing to do just then, but the thought of all those guns in that closet at the villa brought him to his senses and put a damper on any romantic inclinations. "Don't you think somebody back at the house will wonder where you are? Maybe we better go back there."

"No, I want to go to a movie."

Elbow sighed. "Okay, where's the nearest movie theater?"

"It's at the mall. I used to go there a lot before...before Carlo. I'll show you the way." She indicated which way to turn. "You drive real slow. I would be there by now."

"Yeah, those little speed limit signs are ridiculous. Slows the traffic down." Elbow said and looked at her. She didn't get the sarcasm but he didn't expect her to. This was going to be a long day. The mall theater parking lot was busy for the afternoon matinees, but he found a spot near the door.

Anita was excited as she got out of the car. "I haven't been here in a long time. They jazzed the place up with lights and all and changed the sign out front," she almost giggled.

"What movie do you want to see?" He asked "They got an X-Man, two romances, a Star Wars and something animated with penguins."

"I don't care. Which one do you want?"

"Star Wars."

"Okay, let's see that one."

Elbow bought tickets. She wanted popcorn and a drink too. The opening trailers were just starting when they entered the large theater. Thundering sound they could feel through their feet rumbled off the screen while flashes of explosions from a war flick trailer lit up the darkness. They found seats halfway up, and settled in. The rest of the seats filled up fast.

Anita's eyes were glued to the screen. Elbow's eyes scanned their immediate area. Another couple sat next to them and a small family sat behind. No worries. It had been ages since he had been to a movie too. He leaned back into the comfy seat to enjoy the show.

Anita kept the bucket of popcorn to herself and didn't share. Due to unforeseen circumstances, Elbow was used to gaps in his eating schedule and wasn't really hungry. She was self-absorbed and not used to sharing anything.

The movie began with the usual fast action scenes and plenty of booming, soundtrack explosions. Anita momentarily stopped eating popcorn. She seemed to like the movie bodies flying into deep space, which was a little disturbing.

The action slowed a bit as the adventure plot with strange characters emerged. The kid behind her, maybe six or seven years old, got bored with the lack of explosive carnage and started kicking the back of Anita's seat.

"Stop that!" Anita said rather loudly. Several people around her responded with shushing sounds. The kid stopped for about five seconds then continued. His parents were either so engrossed in the movie they didn't notice or they didn't care.

Anita turned to Elbow. "Make him stop."

Elbow looked behind him. The kid was enjoying beating up the back of Anita's seat. His father was a rather large man who might take exception to someone stopping the kid's soccer practice on Anita's headrest. Judging by the lightning tattoos on her bare arms, the kid's mother looked as if she was the more formidable of the parents.

Elbow tried the polite approach. "Ah, could you maybe save the kicking for after the movie?"

"You talkin' to my kid?" the man said.

"Yeah, the lady would appreciate it if he would stop kicking the seat."

"Don't talk to my kid."

"Sure, I'll talk to you then. Could you suggest that junior here stop kicking the seat?"

"No. Mind your own business, dorkhead. Leave the kid alone."

Anita was getting upset. "Aren't you going to shoot him or give him a bloody nose or something?"

"Who? The kid?"

"No, his big fat father!"

This was getting ugly. Anita had no filters in her brain, no sense of what winds people up and makes them want to strangle her. The fact that she didn't remember Elbow didn't have a gun or even that it would be terrible to pull a gun in a crowded movie theater much less shoot it, escaped her limited sense of logic. The kid's dad might even have a gun in his waistband or the mom might have anything up to a bazooka in her over-sized handbag. Heck, even the kid might be carrying. Time to exit the building before someone kicked more than the back of her seat.

Elbow got up and pulled Anita up to escort her out to the aisle. "Hey, what do you think you're doing? I want to see the movie!" she yelled.

"Sorry, we don't want to start a riot with the kid's father."

"That big tub of lard?" She pulled her hand free and the container of popcorn went sailing through the air, scattering buttered popcorn all over the kicker's family behind them.

Time to exit fast and get a head start before dad could pry himself out of his seat and follow them. Anita protested all the way as Elbow wrapped his arm around her waist and almost carried her down the stairs and out the door into the hallway. The guy wouldn't be too far behind.

CHAPTER 35: QUICK CHANGE

Emergency situations call for emergency solutions. Because the hallway was long and the guy could easily see them if they ran, Elbow pushed Anita into the men's restroom across from the theater.

"Just what do you think you're doing?! Let go of me!" She yelled.

He put his hand over her mouth. "Sorry to do this but the kid's dad is as mad as it gets, and if you scream he will find us and maybe put a bruise or two on your pretty face. So if you don't want that then I suggest you stay quiet and we'll just stay safe in here until he cools down, okay?"

Her eyes grew wide as she suddenly comprehended what was going on. She nodded. Elbow slowly took his hand away from her mouth and put his finger to his lips to indicate she was to keep quiet. He motioned for her to stay where she was as he ventured around the corner to see what was happening.

The man was lumbering down the hallway away from them in the direction of the entrance. He might even get the management or security involved, but he didn't seem to be a law and order type and would probably try his own form of justice first.

The movie in the theater next door ended and a wave of people filled the hallway. It was a lucky break. Elbow motioned for Anita to follow him and they joined the flow of the mass as it exited into the mall.

"Hey, Dad! I see them!" The kicker kid yelled. "They went out that door."

Elbow grabbed Anita's hand and hurried her deeper into the mall, along a row of store windows, as fast as her tight skirt and five-inch heels would allow. Around the first corner he spotted a sporting goods store. Perfect. He almost dragged her inside and immediately went to the back where they would be hidden by displays of jeans and sports jerseys.

She curled up her lip in disgust. "Why did you bring me in here? This is all sports stuff. It's not my style!"

"I know it isn't, but this *stuff* is going to get us out of here in one piece. What size are you?"

"You actually want me to wear this?"

"Yes. Look, we are both very visible, especially you in that red sequined outfit."

"I like sequins."

"Yeah, real pretty, but if you wear that making a rush to the car, the guy or his wife will spot you. If we look like the rest of the mall crowd we'll be invisible. Got it? What size?"

"You're really pushy, you know that?"

"Sorry, but I didn't call the guy a 'lard butt' and douse him with buttered popcorn to get him all riled up. What size or do I have to guess?"

"The popcorn was an accident."

"Sure. What size?"

"Two."

Elbow enlisted the aid of a sales girl to help Anita. He picked out a pair of fashionably worn jeans for himself, a couple of team jerseys—Buccaneers for him, Dolphins for her—two baseball caps, and sneakers for each of them. He changed into his outfit, paid for everything and asked the sales girl to cut off the tags.

When Anita emerged from the dressing room and looked into the store mirror she was not a happy camper. The jersey was oversized so she tied the bottom in a knot at the side. Elbow pulled her long, dark hair tucked it under the baseball cap.

"I look like crap. What if I see someone I know?"

He threw her a pair of sunglasses. "In this outfit, even your own grandmother wouldn't recognize you. But it will get us past the kicker's family. They won't recognize you either. That's the point. And you might want to ditch the big earrings and the fancy watch."

"But these are my favorites."

He held open the shopping bag that held the rest of her clothes and she begrudgingly took off the jewelry. They left the store and disappeared into the crowd of shoppers to make their way to an exit door to the parking lot.

As they turned the last corner, they were almost home free. Elbow suddenly grabbed Anita's waist and turned her to look in a store window.

"Hey, what are you doing?" She asked and tried to pull away.

"Don't look up. Dad is right behind us off to your left. Keep looking in the window," Elbow whispered and pointed to a display of air conditioners.

Dad walked right by them. As soon as it was clear, they strolled at a leisurely pace out the exit door and headed for the car.

"You were right. He didn't see us at all!" Anita gushed. "How do you know all this stuff?"

"I don't like getting beaten up or in this case getting you beaten up. Seriously, Anita, you might want to dial down the tone of some of your comments. People don't respond well to being insulted."

"But it was the truth. He was a lard butt. And his kid was a pain in the ass. And his mother looked like she ran a tattoo parlor."

"Yeah, maybe, but you might want to *think* those comments instead of spouting them off. It just might get your teeth knocked in someday when no one is around to protect you."

"You're a mean bastard. You're always criticizing me." She folded her arms and sulked.

"See, you don't like it any more than anyone else."

"I'll tell Carlo about you, how you roughed me up and talked back to me."

"Yeah, you do that. I'll be out of here by tomorrow anyway.

"You're leaving? I don't want you to leave."

They arrived at the car. "You want to drive or me?"

"You drive." She pouted.

CHAPTER 36: BIG POUT

Back at the villa, Anita continued to sulk. She opened her own car door, left it open for Elbow to close and walked out of the garage, giving him the silent treatment. Elbow gathered up the shopping bags and followed her into the house and up to her suite of rooms.

"Where would you like these bags?" he asked.

She pointed to the sofa. "Now get out. I have to change out of these ugly clothes before anyone sees me."

"You're welcome." Elbow kept walking into the hall and closed the door behind him. A sneaker landed with a big thump on the other side of the door. My goodness the lady was temperamental! One minute she is all giggly at the thought of fooling the kicker family and the next she lapses into her Princess-of-the-Entire-World personality. Time to figure a way to escape the house, the job and crazy Anita without adding to his bruise collection.

He made his way to the back stairs and up to his room. He inspected outside the window to see if there was any possibility of exiting that way. No luck. The window was three stories up with a tall wall, topped with glass shards, ten feet away at the bottom. Even Spider-Man would have trouble with that scenario.

He turned his attention to his new sports duds. They were a good disguise. Only Anita knew what they looked like. They might come in handy sometime for a quick change if he had to run for it. He took a shower and dressed in the black silk shirt and dark pants. Back down the stairs, he found the kitchen.

One of the other muscle suits was busy chowing down on tacos. Elbow nodded. The guy nodded back and stuck out his hand.

"Roberto." He continued eating.

"Elbow," he echoed, and shook the guy's hand.

Cici hurried to serve him his taco dinner. She smiled shyly. The older woman, Concetta, kept her eye on her.

Just as Elbow began to eat, Miguel came into the kitchen. "You're wanted upstairs, Elbow. Now."

Looks like Anita got to the boss already. The you-know-what was about to hit the fan. Damn, the taco was good too. He wiped his chin with the napkin, shoved back his plate and followed Miguel up a short flight of stairs to the splendor of the dining room. The boss sat at one end of the table behind an ornate silver center piece. Anita sat to his right dressed in a shimmery blue number with ruffles around the sleeves. She didn't look at Elbow when he entered the room.

The boss motioned for them to enter. Miguel marched him right up to the head of the table. The boss finished chomping down on his salad, put down his fork and wiped his mouth and chin with a wad of napkin. "So ..., what's this I hear about you givin' Anita here a hard time?"

Elbow squirmed a little under the man's cold gaze. "A hard time? You said to keep her safe. I kept her safe. She doesn't have a bite mark on her."

"She says you were mean to her. I don't put up with guys bein' mean to her."

Elbow sighed. "Well, there was this big construction dude in a burger joint who wanted to talk to her. He got a little close and I had to convince him, sudden like, to lie down on the floor. Then we left and she wanted to go see a movie, so we went to see a movie. A brat sitting behind her kicked her seat. When I asked him to stop his father jumped in. Then Anita—Miss Gonzales—called him a lard butt—"

"No! I said he was a tub of lard."

"Right, and for some reason the guy took offense at that so I started to escort Anita—Miss Gonzales—out of harm's way. Her popcorn suddenly exploded all over the guy, his wife and the kid."

"It was an accident!"

"Sure, an accident, but the guy wasn't happy, as you can imagine. While the guy was busy getting his bulk out of the seat, I took her out of the theater."

"Into the men's bathroom!"

"It was the first available place to hide. Then this big group of people left the theater next door and we slipped out with them to the mall exit. The kid spotted us and the chase was on. She had on this bright red outfit with sequins so I hurried her into a sporting goods store. I know she is used to dressing real sharp, but I explained that her outfit was a little too easy to see and why it would be a bad thing if they caught her and she got clobbered. So we bought some clothes, jeans and jerseys, to wear as a disguise and walked out right under their noses. I admit it wasn't the most graceful exit, and Miss Gonzales is used to dressing more stylishly, but no one got hurt and that's the main thing."

"He was mean to me. He said someday I might get my teeth knocked in if I said things to people."

The boss looked at Elbow and then Anita. "That the way it went?" he asked her.

"Yeah, mostly. But he told me I shouldn't say the guy was a lard butt, and his kid was a brat, and don't get me started on his wife."

The boss laughed. "See, what did I tell you? She's headstrong, you know? I tell you, she's a pistol. You did good, Elbow, but she don't like people tellin' her things even if it's for her own good. We got to keep her happy. Okay?" He laughed again. "Yep, she's a pistol."

Anita pouted and looked away. The boss waved his hand to dismiss Elbow.

In the hallway, Miguel looked at Elbow sideways. "Did you really put down a bruiser in a burger joint?"

"He got a little too close and I sort of made his knee bend backwards."

Miguel laughed. "Hell, you're all right, Elbow. Too bad Miss Gonzales didn't appreciate it."

"Just between you and me, Miguel, I don't think she fully understood what was going on. I got her out of a jam in that movie theater and all she did was gripe about the clothes and give me the stink eye silent treatment. She doesn't have a clue."

Miguel laughed again. "You got that right. She's a sweetheart one minute and can bite your ass the next. Some of it's an act, but she plays it real good."

Elbow made his way back to the kitchen hoping for more tacos, but no luck. It was all cleaned up. He headed back to his room and turned on the TV. There was nothing on except a second-rate sitcom, fifty infomercials, two talking heads arguing politics and a couple of Mexican westerns. He turned it off. What did people do for fun around there? Was there a bar nearby? Did they even go out?

He studied the view from the window again. There had to be a way. Another day saving "Princess Anita" from herself and he might get crushed by an irate sumo wrestler or be a candidate for the loony bin.

He lay down on the bed and stared at the ceiling. Several scenarios flitted through his mind. He suddenly sat up. Bingo! That's it. He laughed. It was so simple. What could go wrong?

CHAPTER 37: HAIR DO

Morning dawned bright and clear. Elbow jumped out of bed. Today was the day. He was getting out. Anita just had to be Anita and it would go off without a hitch.

He got dressed in the black outfit and packed his old jeans, new sports duds, baseball cap and sunglasses in the plastic bag from yesterday. He threw in his aluminum sneakers and the free shampoo and toothbrush from the bathroom. He was ready.

He wound his way to the kitchen, hoping for more coffee cake or maybe even leftover tacos for breakfast. The kitchen was in chaos. Cici had just dropped a tray headed for Anita's bedroom and Concetta was giving her hell for it. The poor girl was in tears, trying to pick up the remains of broken dishes, spilled coffee, and juice off the floor. Elbow knelt down to help pick up the pieces. Concetta disapproved but didn't interfere.

"No, no, *señor*. I do this," Cici tried to tell him through the tears.

Elbow gave her a friendly grin and shoveled most of the mess into a trash can. Cici followed with a mop and hurried to replace the breakfast on the tray.

"Put that tray down," Concetta told her. "You can't go upstairs to serve breakfast sniveling and weeping like that. Miss Anita won't like it."

"I'll take it," Elbow volunteered. "I have to talk to her anyway." He picked up the tray and left the kitchen before Concetta had a chance to object. Actually, he was interested to see what mood the Princess was in. The more ticked off she was the better. He reached her door and knocked.

"Come in." Anita grumbled. She was in bed surrounded by silk sheets and rich curtains. She was without make up and her hair was tangled. " What are you doing here?" she yelled. "Where's that girl, Cici?"

"Just helping out," he replied. "There was a minor catastrophe in the kitchen this morning. Are you going shopping this morning?"

"Get out! I'll tell you when I want to go shopping or do anything else!"

Elbow gave her a little bow, turned around and left. She was in fine form. Perfect.

Back in the kitchen. Cici had laid out a lovely display of breakfast things for Elbow. Juice, coffee, pancakes and syrup were all waiting for him. She gave him a shy smile. He thanked her and kept it neutral in case Concetta was taking notes. Concetta told her to fix another tray for the boss and kept an eagle eye on her so nothing else got dropped.

A buzz sounded on the notice board behind him. "Cici, Miss Gonzales is through with her breakfast tray. Go get it," Concetta ordered. "Don't trip this time!" Cici hurried to obey. Concetta was a real gorgon.

Elbow cooled his heels and waited until her majesty, Anita, was ready to go out and beat up another part of the world. Her schedule said she had an appointment at the beauty salon. His phone went off around eleven and he headed for the garage. It was showtime.

Anita displayed a silent, aloof attitude, probably just to show him who was boss as he opened the car door for her. She drove with her usual disregard for the rules of the road. Elbow worked hard to keep his impulse to grab onto something in check. He was going to look calm if it killed him, and with the way she drove, that was a real possibility.

They arrived at the beauty salon intact. She stopped the car in the middle of the street, opened her car door all by herself, got out and threw the keys at him. Oh my, she was pissed!

Elbow found a parking spot just three spaces farther down the street and parked the car. He entered the beauty salon and went through the motions of looking for suspicious characters. He found none and settled in near the front desk.

The receptionist behind the counter was a bleach blond, about twenty-five and made-up to the hilt. She would do nicely for his plan. At first Elbow admired her with his eyes. The girl noticed, but kept it cool and professional. She offered him coffee. He accepted with a smile. She swiveled off to the coffee machine, poured a cup and gave it to him with a smile. He thanked her and smiled. He politely admired her perfume and they were off. He kept it chatty and got her to laugh.

Anita was sitting in a salon chair with her back to him. He could feel her eyes observing him in the mirror. Time to turn it up a notch. He got up from his chair and leaned on the desk to talk to the girl. She crossed her legs, leaned forward and twirled a lock of her hair with her fingers. They were having a grand time.

Elbow snuck a peek at Anita. Her hair was wrapped around giant rollers and she was headed for the hair dryer. He noticed she held a magazine just below the level of her eyes, so she could keep watch on the desk every once in a while.

The receptionist took care of a few phone calls and escorted a couple of patrons to their waiting stylists. Elbow made sure to trail his eyes up and down the blond's figure as she walked back and forth. He was enjoying his little drama.

Well roasted from the dryer, Anita sat back in the salon chair. Her hair was brushed and arranged to perfection and spritzed with enough hairspray to make a dent in the ozone layer. Beauty mission accomplished, she tipped the stylist and headed for the desk to settle the bill.

Elbow put on his serious, working face and stood ready for orders as she approached. She ignored him and didn't look at the receptionist either. Elbow made sure to open the salon door for her then turned and winked at the blond as he went out.

Anita held out her hand for the keys. "Where is it?" she demanded.

Elbow pointed up the block three spaces. Anita walked straight to the car. Elbow matched her hurried steps and opened the car door for her. She got in and started it up before he was even in his seat. He barely had time to close his door before she screeched off into traffic.

CHAPTER 38: TRUTH OVERLOAD

"You seem in a hurry today, Miss Gonzales. More shopping?" Elbow asked calmly. She made a fast, left turn that shoved him up against the car door. He tried to act nonchalant as she straightened the car out and he slid back into place.

She pulled into the parking lot of a fancy clothing store. "You're a bastard sleaze bag, that's what you are!" She growled at him.

"I beg your pardon, ma'am. Have I done something to offend you?" He gave her his most innocent look.

"Yes, and don't call me ma'am, you make me sound like an old lady."

"Certainly, Miss, anything you say."

"Yesterday you weren't very nice to me," she pouted.

"And last night I got called on the carpet by the boss because you complained I treated you 'roughly'. The truth is I saved your ass twice yesterday, but maybe I didn't curtsy enough when I did it."

"There you go again! You're being mean to me. And you were making google-eyes at that receptionist!"

He was almost afraid she was going to cry. "Miss Gonzales, what in the hell do you want from me? The receptionist was just being friendly. I'm human. I was just being friendly back."

"It looked like more than that to me. Did you tell her that her hair looked nice? You didn't tell me my hair looked nice."

Sweet holy pancakes, the woman was nuts. "The receptionist didn't try to drive off down the street when I was barely inside the car."

"You say mean things," she pouted.

"Sorry. My job is to keep you safe, but you don't make that easy. One minute you want your boyfriend, Carlo, to chew me up because maybe I tell you the truth and the next you treat me like dirt when I am super polite and don't say anything."

"I don't know what you mean!" She said with a super-pout and turned away from him.

"Sure you do. Maybe you've lived in that lux villa too long. You have the world served up on a plate every day and you're not happy. Is that why you take it out on me?"

"Get out! Get out of the car!" she yelled.

"No ma'am. My job is to sick with you."

She started the car, put it in gear and roared out of the parking lot. It was all Elbow could do to hang on as she drove the red Maserati through a couple of quiet streets and made a sharp right into the alley next to the villa. She put on the brakes and came to a jarring halt just inches from the garage door. She sat there looking at the door. "I'll tell Carlo about you," she said.

"Good, maybe he'll fire me, but don't lay it on too thick, I'd like to leave without dodging bullets."

She pouted again and turned to look at him. "I don't want you to leave."

"Why?"

"Because ... because I like you. It was so nice in the park when you talked to me. You talked to that receptionist like that. Why don't you talk to me all the time like that?"

She was suddenly getting 'cozy'. This was not going the way he planned. Time for a more direct approach. "Why? Because one minute you're nice as pie and the next you treat me and everyone else like a dog you order to sit up, roll over and play dead."

"I do not!"

"Oh yes, you do."

"Do not!"

"You have a nasty little temper and you bite everyone in the shins with it when you don't get your way. There's a cure for that, but it involves a good spanking and a time out without caviar for dinner!"

She swung her hand at his face. He ducked and she ended up hitting the headrest. Whatever she was trying to do, it wasn't working for her and she was pissed.

Maybe he laid it on a little too thick. Time to grab his stuff and make an exit any way he could before Carlo got an earful from her point of view and sent the muscle troops after him.

Anita hit the garage door opener, wheeled the red beast into the garage and slammed it into park. She left the engine running, got out and almost kicked the door closed. Elbow turned the car off before anyone got carbon monoxide poisoning and headed for the back stairs.

He sprinted up to the top level, grabbed the plastic bag with his stuff, and started back down the stairs. It wouldn't be long before Carlo's men mobilized and came looking for him. That wasn't part of the plan.

He could hear heavy footsteps running in the hall below. Damn! She got to the heavy muscle. He turned around and sprinted back up the stairs.

CHAPTER 39: SWEET CICI

It wasn't part of the plan for Anita to get so worked up. Why, oh why didn't he keep his mouth shut? He had met his share of nutty women, but she topped them all. Anita just had a way of setting him off and he couldn't resist giving her an earful. Oh well, it was too late now.

His goal was to make it to the garage where he could maybe get one of the doors open so he could slip out. He would have stayed in the garage earlier but he needed to get his plastic bag of stuff.

Damn stuff! It was just clothes, but it was all he had. He could be gone by now. He could have been gone yesterday. He should have run off with the dog.

Where the heck could he hide? The first thing Carlo's posse was going to do was check his room, so that was out. He looked down the hall and spotted Cici coming out of her room. Her face lit up when she saw him. The gods of mercy were looking down on him. He smiled back. "Cici, Carlo's men are after me. Hide me in your room until they pass. Please!"

She opened the door and let him in. She motioned for him to hide under the bed. He could just barely peek at the door from his hiding place. She opened the door again. What the hell was she doing? Miguel and the men ran past!

"You see that Elbow guy go by here?" Miguel asked.

She just looked down the hallway in the opposite direction and pointed. Clever girl!

"Thanks," Miguel said and the posse thundered off.

She closed the door and walked over to the bed. "You come out now," she whispered.

"Thanks, that was close," Elbow said as he crawled out from under the bed.

"Why they chase?" she asked.

"I sort of told Anita she was nuts."

Cici put her hand over her mouth to suppress a laugh. "*Si,* she nuts, but she no like to hear."

"No. Look, I got to get out of here. If I can make it down to the garage I can maybe make the door open and get out."

"You can get out?"

"Yes, but they can't see me."

"I want out too. I get you there, you take me with?"

"This must be a pretty good job right now. Why do you want to leave?"

"They bring me here in truck. Say I work but they no pay."

"Where are you from?"

"Guatemala. They promise, but no green card. They not nice."

"Holy Mike. You're an illegal. They're trafficking! Maybe that's his business..."

"I go with?"

"Sure, but with two of us, we got to do it right. Pack a bag, like a plastic bag, only light stuff, nothing you can't carry, and hide me someplace downstairs. Fix dinner as usual and after dinner we'll find a way to get out."

"I go too? You promise?"

"Yeah, sure, tonight, okay? But play it cool until then."

Cici hurried to put her meager possessions in a plastic bag. Elbow opened the hallway door a crack and listened closely for Carlo's men. The coast was clear. Elbow and Cici carefully descended the stairs to the kitchen. It was empty.

Cici motioned for him to follow her to a locked door in the hallway. She pointed above them to the camera aimed at the back door. Elbow understood. If he hugged the wall next to the door, he would not be visible when she opened it. It didn't matter if the camera could see Cici. It would look like she was just doing her job.

Cici opened the door with a key and turned on the light. It was a deep closet, maybe five or six feet, that held mops, brooms, a vacuum cleaner, and a couple of large plastic trash bins. She motioned for him to follow. She closed the door to the hallway and walked up to the shelves at the back of the closet. She pulled on one of the hooks that held a mop. There was a soft click and the shelf wall slid back a few inches. A secret door.

"We be quiet," she whispered. Behind the door was a short flight of steps leading down to another door. This one was steel with rivets on it like the bulletproof back door. Elbow figured whatever was behind it wasn't a trash can that needed emptying, but something valuable that needed extra protection.

As they walked down the stairs, the shelf wall behind them clicked shut. Cici again signaled to watch out for the camera above them aimed at the steel door at the bottom of the stairs. Whoever designed the security system didn't put much thought into which way the doors opened. It was entirely too easy to sneak past and enter once the doors were open and blocked the view.

Cici punched a few numbers into the keypad. The metal door hinges creaked open. The air was filled with a warm, earthy smell. Elbow shivered. He had smelled it before. Birds!

Cici hurried him through the door and closed it behind them. "You hide here. I come after dinner. We go then, yes? You safe here. Miguel, he no like birds." She smiled and left.

Elbow winced at the cacophony of chittering, trilling, clacking, and chirping in the room. He looked at the rows of cages. Was it safe here? Dozens of beady eyes with beaks attached stared down at him, their little bird brains already assessing whether to kill him now or wait until later. His history with birds was not sterling. Every bird he ever had the misfortune to meet had it in for him. Was it bad karma or what? Whatever it was, he hated them back, and here he was trapped in a closed room with a feathered militia.

There were already rumblings of discontent from a rack of cockatoos. Smaller green parrots gripped the sides of their cages with their skinny, clawed feet, chattering their bird taunts to stir up the rest. At least they were still in cages and not loose.

They were all part of a bird trafficking operation. Maybe there were other animals like snakes and panthers there too. They were all trapped in cages, ready to be sold to people who didn't have a clue how to take care of them. Elbow almost felt sorry for them, but then he remembered they were birds, his arch enemy.

The bird chatter began to reach a high pitch. Better do something to calm it down before someone other than Cici showed up. He spotted a bag of seeds in the corner. Maybe the feathered fiends could be bribed to shut up with seeds.

He grabbed a handful of seeds and threw it toward the cages. There was an instant crescendo of noise and then silence as the birds discovered the seed bounty and chowed down. Other birds in the back row complained about not receiving their fair share so Elbow tossed more seeds until everyone was satisfied and all he could hear was crunching.

Crunching was good. It wasn't screeching. Maybe if he fed them enough they would all overeat and fall into a stupor. There was a watering can in the corner along with the seeds. Might as well load them down with water too. Trying to avoid eye contact, he moved carefully between the cages slopping water into their little bowls. Several smaller birds took a break from crunching and tended to basic hygiene, splashing water with great enthusiasm on their neighbors. It was contagious. Soon all the birds were whooping it up and the air was filled with feathers and a fine mist of water. Elbow retreated to a relatively dry corner and sat on the bag of seeds. After their initial frenzy of the communal shower, the birds settled down to grooming feathers and tending to their toenails.

Elbow reasoned that if he sat still, the bird brigade might forget about him and stay quiet. No such luck. Refreshed and alert, they were at it again. He couldn't stand it. Anything was better than several dozen mouthy birds killing his eardrums. He had to get out even if he ran into Miguel.

He ran his hand over the steel door. A small nob protruded from one side. He pushed it. The door popped open a crack. He heard noises in the closet at the top of the stairs. Someone was checking it out. Next they would be inspecting the bird room. He had a crazy idea. So crazy it just might work.

He silently closed the steel door. Taking his life in his hands, he started opening cages. Smaller birds flew out and perched on other cages. He left his arch enemies, the cockatoos, for last. Feathers floated in the air as the birds flew everywhere, testing their freedom. He squeezed himself into the corner near the door and turned out the light. The birds fell silent in the darkness. A key turned in the lock with a *snick*. The door opened. The bright stairway light shone into the room like a beacon, silhouetting a figure in the doorway.

At first the birds were stunned by the light in the pitch black of the room. They recovered quickly. Light meant freedom. In a mad burst of wings and screeching, the birds made their move and rushed the doorway. The man fell backward and banged his head on the steel door. He was out cold. Birds filled the stairway. Elbow saw his chance and took it, racing past the prone figure to the top of the stairs along with the birds. The door to the closet and the door to the hall stood open. The birds made the most of it, streamed through it and flew in every direction.

He heard screaming from the kitchen. The birds had made it that far and maybe even up the stairs to the second floor. The guy at the bottom of the stairs started to recover and soon the full force of Carlos' army would muster, but they would be preoccupied with corralling the birds.

He could hear footsteps thundering down the stairway above him.

There was no time to escape from the closet. They had already searched the closet so maybe they wouldn't search it again. Elbow sized up the available hiding places and quickly slid into place under a shelf behind the large, plastic, trash bins. The space was cramped and claustrophobic, but at least he was invisible and free from the birds. He settled in to wait.

It's strange what you hear when there is nothing else to do. There were hurried footsteps overhead on the stairs above the closet. Doors opened and shut with a loud bang. There was shouting. Several sets of feet hurried past the closet door to and from the locked back door. They were having a grand time collecting all the birds.

He looked around the dim closet for anything he could use as a weapon in case they found his hiding place. He carefully reached up to the shelf above him. There were several bottles of cleaning products where a splash or two might distract an intruder long enough so he could whack a sensitive place with a broom handle. It wasn't the best plan but it would have to do.

Elbow caught himself dozing off in the closet, in spite of all the noise and running back and forth and captured birds squawking, as people trudged past him down the stairs to the cages. Normally he wouldn't mind taking a snooze or two during the day but maybe not in a cramped closet. The sound of voices brought him back to a state of alert. It was Miguel and one of the posse.

"This is the last of them." Miguel shook his head. "If I never see another feather..."

"Yeah. Too bad we can't shoot 'em," said the posse guy. "I hate birds. How the hell did they get out in the first place?"

"I'll give you one guess," Miguel said.

"That Elbow guy?"

"Yeah. When we find him I hope they give me first whack at him. That big white one pooped on my suit and bit me."

Elbow smiled. Universal karma at its best. One of the cockatoos bit Miguel and gave him a guano salute.

They turned off the light and used a key to lock the closet. Time passed slowly in the dark closet. There was no telling what time it was except for the smell of something cooking in the kitchen. Elbow was hungry and the aroma was driving him crazy. Maybe Cici would save him something for later.

Sounds from the kitchen increased as Carlo's herd showed up to get their turn at the feed trough. He hoped Cici kept her cool and didn't appear nervous.

Sounds suddenly spilled out into the hallway. Elbow went on high alert and made himself as small as possible under the shelf. The closet door opened and the light flipped on. He held his breath. It was Cici ... and someone else.

"Miguel, you no help," she teased. "I can do all by myself."

"No trouble, Cici."

"No, no. I take trash in here. You no spoil you nice shirt," she giggled. "Oh, I forget bag in kitchen."

"I'll get it for you, hon," Miguel said.

Elbow smirked. Miguel was sweet on Cici.

"Hurry," Cici whispered. "Get in trash can."

"How did you know I was here?"

"You shoe. I see it stick out under shelf. Miguel, he no see."

Whatever she had in mind, it was not the time to argue. Elbow quickly crawled out from the cramped space under the shelf and climbed into the large, rolling trash bin. As soon as he was in the bottom of the bin, Cici tossed their plastic clothing bags on top of him. Miguel returned from the kitchen with a bag of kitchen waste and Cici tossed it casually into the top of the bin and flipped the lid closed.

The bottom of the bin smelled suspiciously like tacos and old coffee grounds. Elbow suddenly realized Miguel must be pushing the bin. The muscled Romeo was actually helping them escape. Clever little Cici. She was far more intelligent than anyone gave her credit for. The bin stopped rolling. Elbow imagined they were at the back door to the alley and Miguel was punching numbers in the keypad. He heard the door click open. The bin moved again, bumping down the back steps with bruising punishment and rumbled across the cobblestones to the dumpster.

"Oh, you so strong," Cici said.

Miguel was distracted. Cici began moving the plastic bags from the bin to the dumpster.

"Here, let me help you with that," Miguel told her.

"No, you too pretty in you suit. You get all dirty," she told him.

"My suit's got bird poop on the back."

"Oh, the birds, they scare me all over the kitchen. You bring suit to kitchen later. I clean."

"That's real sweet of you, honey," Miguel said. His phone went off. He said a few words and turned rapidly to re-enter the building.

"Carlos is pissed. One of the birds did a nasty number on his desk. They're going through the house room by room. We'll find that Elbow guy. He's not in your room, is he?" He laughed.

Cici blushed. "Oh no, he not in my room."

"Sorry I got to go. I'll leave the door open a crack, but be sure to close it tight when you come back in with the can," Miguel said as he hurried through the back door.

"I never go back in that door again," Cici said under her breath. She tapped on the side of the garbage bin. "You okay, Mr. Elbow?"

"Yeah, just a little dented on one side. Everything clear?"

"*Si.* Miguel, he go back in door. You hurry now. Someone maybe see here with camera."

Cici tipped the trash bin on its side. Elbow crawled out dragging the two plastic bags with him. Cici took off her apron and threw it in the dumpster. Elbow grabbed the two bags and Cici's arm and headed up the alley at a fast trot. If someone was monitoring the security TV screens, the posse would be on them in a flash. Time to move and find a safe place to change clothes so they would be invisible and could put some distance between themselves and the villa.

The main street was just ahead. Even though he had whipped past the shops at warp speed earlier when Anita was driving, he remembered a fruit stand and some sort of store with Mexican hats and colorful rugs hanging outside. A quick look confirmed his memory.

"Cici, we're too visible in these clothes. Here, put on this shirt."

"It bright red!"

"Yeah, but look around. Everything on this block shouts color. In black we stand out like a blinking sign." She slipped the red shirt on over her black dress. "Take your hair down too."

"Concetta make me wear it up in kitchen."

Elbow smiled. "You're not in the kitchen anymore."

She smiled and her eyes turned bright.

"They probably don't know we're gone yet, but it's best to be safe."

She undid the comb on top of her head and her silken mane of black hair cascaded down on her shoulders. Elbow admired it.

"You got any different shoes in your bag?" He asked.

"The floppy flips?"

"Yes, flip-flops. Perfect. Get rid of the orthopedic wedgies and put them on."

She grabbed the flip-flops and tossed the black shoes in the plastic bag. Her transformation complete, Elbow ducked behind a stack of bright carpets, took off his black silk shirt and replaced it with the turquoise team shirt he used to escape from the mall the day before. He rolled up the cuffs on his black slacks to just below the knee, put on the new baseball cap and tennis shoes, and presto! He was invisible among the customers inspecting the tomatoes and peaches.

Cici giggled. Elbow laughed too.

CHAPTER 42: INVISIBLE

Tires screeched as a black car roared around the corner from the alley. Elbow turned Cici around. "Quick, look at the apples, not the car! He busied himself thumping cantaloupes as the car slowed mid-block and gave the crowd of shoppers a passing glance. Satisfied, the car roared off.

Cici giggled again. "They no see us!"

"Yeah, but they'll be back so we better buy some apples or something so we look like real customers."

"I no got no money."

Elbow reached into his pocket. His stash from babysitting Anita was substantial and still intact. Cici picked out a few apples. Elbow added a large cantaloupe to the bag and paid for it. He thought the cantaloupe might have good weapon potential if they had to defend themselves. He headed back in the direction of the villa.

"No, no! We...I no go back!" Cici complained.

"Relax, if those goons come back here for another look, they won't expect us to be this close. Besides, I just saw a bus roll by and stop in the next block."

"Where it go?"

"Does it matter? Anywhere is better than here, right?"

She looked around, suddenly afraid. He took her hand and gently led her past the alley entrance to the villa and on to the bus stop. They sat on a concrete bench advertising a smiling lawyer with bulging muscles who specialized in personal injury cases.

Several people joined them waiting for the bus. One guy was a little too full of cheap wine. Elbow decided it was a good idea if the overweight guy sat down on the bench before he fell on it. He offered him his seat. The fellow burped and mumbled thanks.

An older woman wearing shoes with pitifully rundown heels arrived. She looked tired. She carried a red mesh bag filled with odd, lumpy, green fruit. Elbow thought, whatever those things were, they must be on sale. Cici stood up and offered the woman her seat.

A young woman with a tired and irritable three year old arrived. It was all the young mother could do to contain the kid as he pretended to be superman again and again, jumping off the bench onto the sidewalk.

Cici kept glancing in the direction of the alley. Her face was ashen. Her eyes were full of fear. "I can no go back to villa or my country," she whispered. "People in house say I can no go or I go to jail and send me back. I no got papers."

"Yeah, maybe they'll send me somewhere too. I can't exactly prove who I am either. Just pretend you belong here. It's up to them to prove you don't. Besides, you could blow the whistle on the boss and Anita and spoil their whole operation. The government might like that and decide you were a good citizen. That's probably why Miguel and the boss are looking for us. It'll be okay. If I can get back to my old neighborhood, I know a guy who can maybe help with papers, if he's not in jail."

Cici smiled. "You nice to me, Mr. Elbow. I maybe make tacos for you."

Elbow gave her a big smile. The thought of tacos reminded his stomach it was empty and would soon be vocalizing its discontent. "How about breaking out one of those apples, Cici, in all the excitement, I missed both lunch and dinner."

Cici gave him the plastic bag. Elbow selected an apple, but before he could take a bite, the black car appeared again in the next block, driving slowly past all the stores. Elbow spotted it. "Cici, the men are back, coming up the street in the car. Don't look at them."

She couldn't help it. It was just human nature to want to look, and that's when the car took an interest in the park bench and pulled up next to it.

The car door opened. Miguel stepped out. He did not look pleased. "Well, there you are. Get in the car, Cici. You too, bird boy!"

Elbow grabbed Cici's arm and whispered, "Stay here. Make him come to you." He casually slipped his fingers around the handles of the plastic bag of apples with the cantaloupe.

Miguel took a step toward them and slipped his hand inside his jacket. "You heard me. Get in the car."

"No!" Cici said loudly. "You want kidnap me! I no work for you like a slave no more!"

Everyone on the bench riveted on Miguel and the black car. Miguel made a move toward Cici. The bratty little kid, oblivious to the drama unfolding before them, jumped off the bench with perfect timing, right onto Miguel's foot.

Elbow saw his chance. He swung the plastic bag of fruit around his head to get it going and smashed the business end of the cantaloupe right into the side of Miguel's head. The sound it made was a very satisfying *BWONK*. Even more satisfying was seeing Miguel pass out and hit the sidewalk like a felled sequoia.

The back doors of the car swung open. Two guys with guns drawn emerged in rapid fashion. The wine soaked fellow on the bench thought he would stand up and join the fun, but standing up was not the best idea. Elbow could see it before it happened. The guy had trouble deciding which way was up and fell into the first gunman. His stomach followed inertia and unloaded a whole lot of bad wine mixed with what might have been chili onto the guy's nice black silk suit. The look on the silk suit's face was pure shock. The heavyset drunk passed out, took the suit down with him to the sidewalk, and pinned him there with his dead weight in a swamp of vomit. Now there was just the other gunman and the driver.

A bus pulled up behind the black car and sounded its horn in an irritated manner. The black car was in the way. The distraction was just enough. Elbow felt joy rise up in his heart. He grabbed the old lady's red mesh bag off the bench, whipping the lumpy green fruit around his head.

The guy from the back seat ducked to avoid getting smashed like Miguel. But Elbow wasn't aiming for his head. His target was the gun in the guy's right hand. Wham! He scored a direct hit. The guy's fingers crumpled. The gun went off. The bullet skimmed the back of the bench six inches from the old woman, and the lumpy green fruit broke open, scattering its green guts all over the sidewalk. The old woman rose to her feet and began beating the gunman with her cane. The car's driver came to the gunman's rescue. He slipped on the green goo and crashed to the pavement. She beat him too, adding a torrent of words that would have made a convention of bikers blush. Go grannie go!

Elbow grabbed Cici's hand and pulled her toward the black car. The doors were open and the motor was still running. "Get in!" he yelled.

She crawled into the front seat. Elbow hurriedly slammed the door shut and vaulted over the hood to the driver's side. "Seatbelt!" He said as he grabbed his own seatbelt, shoved the car into drive, pressed the gas pedal to the floor and took off.

Cici's hands gripped the arm rest and pushed against the dashboard. "Slow down, Mr. Elbow, I frightened!"

"Sorry, but we just borrowed a car belonging to the boss, Carlos, from some guys with guns. We need to put some distance between us and that mess back there. Whoo-hoo! Did you see that old lady whack those two? I never would have guessed she had it in her."

They heard sirens. He slowed the car to a modest crawl and pulled over as a police car roared past on its way to the bus stop. He made several turns down several blocks to make sure they weren't followed by police or anyone else.

"You good driver, Mr. Elbow," Cici told him.

"Yeah. Too bad I never exactly got around to getting a license." Most of his traveling was by hitchhiking or the generosity of a female driver.

Cici shivered. "Mr. Carlos, he not nice man. Miss Anita, she make him do what she want, but I think she mean sometimes because she not want to be there too. Carlos no like if she go."

"He won't be too happy about the car either. The sooner we get rid of it the better. I know a guy who might take it off our hands for a modest donation. He might even let us watch while he strips it and puts it through the crusher."

Elbow maneuvered the black car through several questionable neighborhoods with pit bulls the neighborhood dog of choice chained up in the front yards. The street soon became semi-industrial. Windows were boarded up or covered with sturdy iron grids. Ritzy neighborhoods gave Elbow the jitters. Now he began to feel right at home.

A tall, worn, wooden fence came into view. Graffiti spray paint decorated most of it and almost obliterated the EDDIE'S SCRAPYARD - NO PARKING sign near the chain link gate. Elbow pulled up on the narrow apron, got out and spoke into the speaker. "Hey, Eddie, It's me, Elbow. I got a car that might need your special attention. You interested?"

"Elbow? You mangey turd, where you been hiding? A bunch of people been lookin' for you."

"Yeah, I kind of had to move around a bit. I got this car. It just sort of fell into my hands and it might need to be scrapped."

"Crap! Is it hot?"

"Not yet, but the owner might not be happy I used it."

"Okay. Bring it in."

CHAPTER 44: EXCHANGE

The gate lock buzzed open and a rusty motor dragged the metal gate to one side. Elbow got back in the Maserati and drove into the yard. The gate motor strained to put the heavy gate back in place and the lock clanked shut behind them.

"Stay in the car, Cici. I'll see what I can do," Elbow told her.

The car pulled up to the office which was covered with an impressive collection of dented, chrome hub caps. The large, greasy figure of Eddie appeared in the doorway. "How you doin', Elbow. Haven't seen you since that thing at the Flamingo."

"How are you, Eddie?"

"Can't complain." Eddie shook his hand. "Pretty fancy car. You movin' up in the world?"

"Not really. You wouldn't maybe want to trade me this for something less...ah...conspicuous?"

"I got a couple of beaters, but It's a mighty pretty car. It got a history?

"Yeah, someone you might not want to meet in a dark alley owns it. You don't want to keep it."

"Drugs involved?"

"Hell no. You know I never been into that crap. Beer is my drug of choice. The car's probably clean, but scraping off the ID numbers might be a good idea before you turn it into a two thousand pound doorstop."

"You gonna tell me about it sometime?"

"Sure, someday when we put back a few dozen beers together, okay?"

Eddie flicked his eyes over the shiny black car. He smiled and extended an oil-stained hand to seal the deal. "Okay. The beaters are around back. Take your pick."

Elbow tossed Eddie the keys. He opened Cici's door to help her out and grabbed the two black plastic bags. Cici looked around at the scrap yard with wide eyes. Behind the ramshackle office building were several small mountains of crushed metal. A large machine was grinding away in one corner, flattening and crunching down a yellow car into an unrecognizable, solid, yellow brick of metal, finally spewing it out onto the stained gravel. A large crane swung overhead, picked up the block with a magnet and neatly added it to a pile of similar blocks of different colors.

"Pretty sweet operation, huh?" Elbow said.

"That what happen to the black car?" she asked.

"Yeah, Eddie's smart enough not to keep it for himself. At least I hope he is."

Elbow looked over the sad collection of used cars behind the office. An old, blue mustang looked less abused than the rest. He kicked the mismatched tires and looked inside. The front seats were still intact. Most of the windows still worked when he tested the engine. One of the taillights had red cellophane taped over it, but the headlights weren't broken and the side mirrors were firmly attached with duct tape. The gas gauge, if it could be believed, said half full. He checked underneath for miscellaneous puddles of oil and other substances and was satisfied it would do. There was even a pine tree air freshener dangling from the rear view mirror.

"Okay, we'll take this one," he told Cici. "Stow those bags in back and we'll get out of here."

"Where we go?"

"We can check out my old neighborhood. We might be able to hang out there a few days and get you some paperwork."

Elbow tried the motor again and was pleased to hear it start without too much protest and no smoke belching from the tailpipe. He ignored several warning lights flashing on the dashboard. There was nothing vital like brakes or oil to worry about. He popped it in gear. It wasn't the swanky, black beast they arrived in, but in so many ways it was much safer.

Elbow guided the car along the main street, getting the feel of the steering, the brakes and the pickup. You never knew when you might need to test the pickup speed. A squad car with lights blazing zipped past, along with an ambulance, headed in the direction of the bus stop. He pretended to be a good citizen and pulled over to let it pass. He laughed.

"Why you laugh, Mr. Elbow?" Cici asked.

"I just wondered how long it will take the cops and the sanitation department to clean up that mess at the bus stop."

Cici smiled. "You throw fruits pretty good."

"I hope you realize we got lucky when that bus showed up."

"*Si,* we lucky. I no like guns. Fruits is better."

CHAPTER 45: HOME AGAIN

Elbow's old neighborhood hadn't changed much. No big developers had tried to gentrify it, it was still a comfy collection of abandoned warehouses and small storefront businesses, tattoo parlors, a couple of rescue missions, and bars.

He drove slowly past his favorite watering place, the Flaming Flamingo bar. The gaudy pink sign with the dancing flamingo legs was dark. The parking lot was empty, and there was a FOR SALE sign tacked on the wall. The Flamingo was an institution. How could it be for sale?

The back of the building held the answer. It was a charred mess. What the fire didn't damage, rain from the latest hurricane finished off. Small trees sprouted in the parking lot and billiard balls were scattered everywhere. Seeing the place in this state almost made him weep. Where else could a guy find a decent place to drink with buddies, shoot a little pool and sweet talk consenting ladies? He wondered if the abandoned warehouse where he once lived had met a similar fate.

He drove the Mustang down a familiar alley and turned into the warehouse truck yard. Everything looked the same. The windows were still stained with rust from the roof. The metal door was a bit more dented but still in place.

He parked the car and got out. Cici joined him. He pulled the doorbell chain that still hung outside and heard the metallic spoons and metal it was attached to upstairs clank. After a minute, the window above the door opened and a familiar red-bearded face peered out.

"Elbow! You old idiot! Where the hell you been?"

"Hi, Red, how are things.?"

"Not bad. Come on in."

A bolt holding the door clicked. Elbow pushed the door open. He motioned for Cici to follow. His eyes quickly adjusted to the dim interior. The floor was still gritty and it all had that musty, industrial smell he remembered. There were several more sheets of plastic hung up around the large, interior space, partitioning it off into rooms.

Red came down the stairs. He still wore the same paint splattered overalls. He shook Elbow's hand. "Good to see you, man. We wondered what the hell happened to you. Last we knew you were in the hospital after the Flamingo thing."

Elbow was not going to bring up the fact that he might have set off the melee that started the brawl and the subsequent fire in the kitchen that brought down the Flamingo. "Yeah, well, I decided it would be healthier if I left town for a while. I headed south."

A curvaceous brunet walked down the stairs wrapped only in a sheet.

"Hey, Tif, come over here. There's someone I want you to meet. This is Elbow. He used to live here. This is Tiffany, my new model."

Tiffany looked Elbow up and down. Elbow gave her an admiring grin. She returned the favor and strolled over to the kitchen area so he got the full effect of her ample hips from the rear.

"So Rosita's not here anymore?" Elbow asked.

"Nah, we had a really big blow up. She set fire to a pile of my paintings and left with that damn bird of hers. After that I sort of rented out the rest of the space to other artists. Thor over there is a sculptor. Andy in the back does jewelry, really far out stuff."

"Anyone in my old space?"

"No. I always thought you might come back one day so I told everyone it was off limits. It's a little dusty but everything is still there. We even added a few luxuries to the bathroom like a washing machine. It's hooked up to a solar panel on the roof that Thor 'found' on the back of a truck."

"All the comforts. Thanks, Red. By the way this is Cici. She...well she needs to stay out of sight until I can find her some papers. Is 'Inks' Donovan still around?"

"Yeah, but let's just say he needed his own special 'identity' services. He grew a beard and dyed his hair and now he's 'Henry O'Day'. He works out of the Lizard Grill down the street."

"That take the place of the Flamingo?"

"Sort of. Most of the regulars are there, but it's not the same."

"Yeah, it's a shame about the Flamingo. Well, I'll get Cici settled in and go scout the place out. Great to see you again, Red."

"You too, Elbow. Stick around for a while. We'll share a beer or two."

"Or six," Elbow said and shook his hand again.

He led Cici over to the faded plastic wall of his old room and peeked in. Everything was still there, just as Red promised. Cici looked at the layers of foam and old exercise mats that did for the bed and the electrical wires hanging down from the steel grid rafters on the ceiling.

"This you place?" She asked, less than impressed.

"Yeah, well, it's not the villa but it beats sleeping in the car. Fix it up if you want. I'm going to the Lizard Grill to see about papers for you. I can bring you back a burger or something."

"*Si*, I hungry."

Elbow rummaged around in the boxes under the bed for some clothes to change into. Somehow they had escaped the invasion of mold and rust from the leaky roof and were still reasonably wearable. He picked out a striped shirt and some jeans with a few miles on them, dressed, got rid of the black silk shirt and pants and felt like a new man.

Elbow walked the three blocks to the Lizard Grill, savoring the atmosphere of familiar places like the Taco Tiki where you could get two greasy tacos for a buck and Raymond's Bail Bonds which had a couple of new bullet holes in the door frame.

The Lizard Grill looked the same too, with enormous steer horns mounted over the door. It attracted a bit rougher crowd than the Flamingo, along with some wannabe guys who dressed like TV cowboys even though there wasn't a steer or a ranch anywhere near south Miami. Elbow preferred company that was more regular, just guys who were wannabe drunks and alcoholics.

He stepped in the door and was greeted by an old, familiar face. It was Ed, the old bouncer from the Flamingo doing the same job patting down customers and keeping order at the Lizard.

"Well, well, well, look what the cat dragged in, Mr. Elbow 'McSwine,'" Ed said as he gave him an extra rough pat down.

"How you doin', Ed?

"You know anything about a motorbike that belonged to my sister? It disappeared about the same time you did."

Elbow put on his Mr. Innocent face and didn't mention that he might have had something to do with it disappearing and now residing on the ocean floor after it disintegrated under him somewhere between Miami and Key West. It was long gone and nobody could prove anything. "Man, she should keep better tabs on that thing. It disappears a lot."

"Yeah," Ed said, unconvinced. "No trouble with you tonight or I might enjoy persuading you to the kiss the sidewalk out front. You got me?"

"Sure, I'm a regular citizen now, Ed. No trouble." Man, the guy was wound up tight. You'd think after all this time the motorbike would be ancient history.

Elbow looked around the main room. There was a little raised stage in one corner where some yodeler was trying to sing and play a guitar but wasn't making much headway against the din of conversation. A girl was giggling as the mechanical bull took her for a ride, dipping and dodging over a padded pit in the middle of the room.

He spotted Inks, alias Henry O'Day, in the last both near the side door, then made his way to the counter and ordered two tall beers. He never would have recognized Inks if Red hadn't clued him in to the new name, beard and hair dye. Inks was deep in conversation with a small Asian man.

Elbow sampled his beer and savored the mellow liquid as it caressed his tastebuds and soothed the sides of his throat on the way down. There hadn't been a lot of opportunity to enjoy the nectar of the gods at the villa. He was a little behind on his quota. The little Asian man left by the side door and Elbow deposited the second beer in front of Inks and sat down opposite him in the booth.

"Elbow?" Inks said. "That really you?"

"Yeah, Inks, that really you?"

"Shh, don't call me that. It's Henry now."

"Sure, sure. Henry it is."

"That beer for me?"

"Yup."

Henry took a healthy sip. "Ah, first one today. I had to cut down. I was gettin' the shakes. That's a bad thing for a guy in my line of work. But one or two steadies the hand, you know?"

"Yeah, moderation is a good thing."

Henry took another healthy sip. "So, I assume this isn't a social call with the beer and all. What can I do for you, Elbow?"

"I need some ID's."

Henry looked around as if someone was about to pounce on him. "For God's sake, Elbow, didn't I never teach you nothin'? You gotta be more subtle. I'm not into that line of work anymore. I do postcards and books."

Henry wanted to talk in code. "Okay. I was wondering if you might have any US postcards for my uh… 'sister'. You know? The kind she likes are green with official looking stamps on them."

Henry smiled and looked interested. "Lotta people interested in those postcards these days. They're rare."

"She might also want a book, the kind with eagles on them."

"Ooh, those aren't on sale this week. Special order only. Shipping would be extra."

"Yeah, I figured that."

"How old's your, uh 'sister'?" Henry asked.

"Twenty-five, I think."

"What was her name? I forgot."

Elbow made one up. "Maria C. Jones."

"Pretty name. You gonna send her postcards and a book for her birthday? That's sweet. When's her birthday?"

"A couple of weeks. The twenty third."

"She's lucky to have a brother like you. By the way, she do much traveling?"

"Yeah, San Diego was her favorite last year."

"Yeah, I never been there but I hear it's nice. I'll see what I can do. Come back tomorrow and buy me another beer."

"Great, nice seeing you again, Henry, take care."

Elbow ambled off to a place near the bar to finish his beer. He saw another man take his place in the booth. Old Henry was doing alright. He looked around the room. No one else was much interested in Henry or the booth, but you could never tell. Fed stuff was tricky. If they were on his trail, Henry would have to do more than select a new hair color, maybe shave close, pick out lipstick and high heels too.

CHAPTER 47: PARTY TIME

Elbow returned to the warehouse with a couple of Lizard burgers. "While you gone I clean," Cici told him. "Mucho dust. I clean you clothes too."

"I was gone an hour, an hour and a half at most. You did all that?"

"I take care of birds at villa. Birds is messy. You more easy. Thor, he say he make me nice bed to sleep."

"Somebody named Thor is already making furniture for you! You have been busy."

"I got no place for sleep. You bed too lumpy. I make Thor tacos."

"What about me? My friend is working on some papers for you."

"For really? Papers? I stay?"

"I hope so. He'll tell me tomorrow."

"I make you tacos too. I make everybody tacos."

"I brought some burgers. They're not tacos but we can have a late lunch."

"No for me. Andy, he give me some sandwich."

Elbow looked at her. She was a little social butterfly. She had already made friends with the warehouse inmates. She went back to cleaning the kitchen area, and Elbow sat down at the card table to make short work of the burgers. They were not the best he had ever eaten. Maybe they really were made of lizards. It was hard to tell. They were dry without a brew or two to wash them down.

He observed that someone, probably Red, had emptied his beer stash, probably to keep it from going past its expiration date, if beer really had an expiration date. He headed out to restock at Billy's Finer Liquors, one of the many establishments serving the local imbibing community.

Billy's didn't waste money on fancy displays or even an abundance of cleaning. It was a no nonsense place with heavy security gates over the doors and windows, ideally suited to the taste and alcoholic preferences of its neighborhood customers. Large packs of beer dominated two whole isles. Wine came in boxes, gallon jugs and even single bottles. Harder choices like scotch and bourbon were behind the counter in smaller, pocket sized containers. No fancy names or labels, just alcohol with the required buzz.

Mrs. Billy sat next to the cash register on a high chair. She was a plus sized woman with a gun on her hip who didn't take kindly to people who messed with her or her merchandise. Elbow made his choice of a couple of twelve packs of one of Milwaukee's finest and got in line at the counter.

"My, my, if it isn't my favorite bad boy returned to the scene of the crime." Mrs. Billy said and smiled, revealing the large gap between her two front teeth.

Elbow smiled back. "How's business, Miranda?"

"Not bad since the Flamingo closed. Had to put in another aisle of beer. Even got some of that fancy, small brewery sap. You havin' a party?"

"No, just stocking up." He gave her another smile and paid the bill.

He wrestled a stray supermarket cart from the tangle behind the dumpster and trekked his bounty back to the warehouse. He parked the borrowed cart next to the door as usual. You never knew when you might need a handy cart to haul things.

The inviting aroma of tacos greeted Elbow as soon as he walked in the warehouse door. Cici had been busy in the kitchen and the residents were starting to assemble for a small feast. Elbow's beer stash took a big hit as the group appropriated his beer as a party offering.

Cici was full of giggles. The source of her giggles was Thor. He spoke to her in Spanish and they obviously had eyes for each other. Elbow was glad to see her happy. He savored his own beer and had a chance to study the other warehouse residents.

Andy, the jeweler, pretty much kept to himself and inhaled tacos like he would never see another meal. He was fond of the beer too. He wore thick glasses and had pale skin as if he spent time in prison and never saw the sun.

Thor was the best of the lot. He had dark, good looks and a very athletic build with shoulders like a linebacker. Some girls like that type. Cici obviously did.

Elbow's eyes were constantly drawn to Red's model, the exotic Tiffany. Oh my, she was fine. His friend, Red, even though he fancied himself a painter, probably made a mess of painting her shimmering skin and flowing curves. He was more a splash and dash type of painter.

Elbow's eyes connected with Tiffany's eyes more than once. She smiled, looked away and crossed her legs. They were lovely legs. Elbow tried hard to resist admiring her attributes but he was never good at resisting. Evidently she wasn't either. She arranged her body so he had the best view. They never exchanged a word, but it was definitely getting interesting.

Elbow consumed the last of the beer, and the party broke up around midnight. The warehouse inmates went back to their plastic, rabbit dens. Cici and Thor took care of cleanup duties. Elbow heard them giggling in the kitchen.

Red needed help managing the stairs up to the second floor. Tiffany lead the way and opened the door while Elbow struggled to keep Red balanced as they negotiated the steel steps one at a time. Finally, Red was deposited spread-eagle on the sofa in his paint studio. He was out for the count.

Tiffany wasted no time. Elbow was done with resisting too. Oh my, she was fine indeed.

Elbow slowly opened his eyes. Where the hell was he? A rusted, metal grid ceiling came into focus above him. Oh yeah, now he remembered. He somehow ended up in Red's bed with Tiffany, the wonder model.

He sat up with a start. Red better not find him there. He hurried to untangle his clothes that were scattered across the floor and struggled to get dressed. His shoes were in the studio/living room next to Red's easel. He tiptoed across the carpet, stuffed his feet in the sneakers without untying them and reached for the door to the stairs. Red had managed to curl up in a fetal position but was still soundly asleep on the sofa. Elbow silently pulled the door open.

"Do you always slink off early in the morning?" A sultry voice behind him said. Tiffany stood in the door to the bedroom with a sheet loosely draped over one shoulder.

Elbow turned around. "No, but this is Red's place and you're Red's model and Red is a friend so I thought it might be polite to be elsewhere when he wakes up."

"Aw, aren't you sweet."

It was one of those smiles. She was one of those women who could melt the bumpers off your car if she wanted to. She moved a step closer. Elbow felt his resistance crumble, again, although to be honest, he didn't put up much of a fight. Red be hanged. The lady was putting out a thousand megawatts of electricity and the sheet was slipping and...

Elbow heard the crunch of gravel as a sleek, black car pulled into the warehouse parking lot.

"Who the hell is that?" Tiffany asked as she strolled over to the window. "Nobody ever comes here."

Elbow looked too. One glance was enough. He pulled her to the side. "No, stay back!"

"They friends of yours?"

"No, and you don't want to know them either."

"Say, who are you? Those guys loan sharks or something?"

"Or something is about right. Look I got to go. You just stay up here and tell them you don't know me or Cici. Got it?"

"What did you do? Rob a bank?"

"I wish! Don't let them in if you can help it and you don't know me. Got it?"

"Sure. It was grand fun last night, Sugar, sure you can't stay?"

He gave her a parting look as if she just tore his heart out and vaulted down the stairs. "Cici! Cici! Wake up! They found us. Get dressed and grab your stuff. We got to get out!"

Cici came out from one of the plastic rooms rubbing the sleep out of her eyes. "We got to go? How they find us?"

"Eddie at the scrapyard probably kept the car and they found it. Hurry."

"Where we go?"

"Anywhere, only just not here. Carlo's men are in the parking lot."

She ran back into the plastic room yelling, "Thor! Thor! They come get me!"

There was pounding on the steel door. "Open up. We know you're in there! You got five minutes, Bird Boy, and then we blast down the door!"

Elbow swore. No time for a graceful exit.

Everyone was up. "What's going on? Is it the police?" Andy asked.

"No. But we gotta go."

Thor came rushing out of one of the plastic rooms. His eyes looked fierce. "We got a plan around here for nosy cops and gate crashers. Everybody get ready! You want to get out of here, Elbow, go ahead, but Cici's staying here!"

Andy and Thor turned rapidly and went back in their work rooms. There was a flash of light as Andy fired up his welding torch behind the plastic.

There was more pounding on the door. "Time's up! We're coming in!"

Good God, Miguel was impatient. It wasn't even five minutes. Thor came out of his plastic room wearing a gas mask and holding what looked like a chainsaw.

"Okay, everybody ready?" Thor yelled.

"Ready!"

"What can I do?" Elbow asked.

"You see Andy's torch? Take it and light up those orange lines over there one at a time when I tell you," Thor said, his eyes wild with some kind of inner fire. "Andy, I need you on the awning. And keep down everyone. This isn't a drill!"

Whatever they had in mind Elbow had second thoughts about handling a welding torch. Maybe he should stay out of the way and try his own plan, but it was too late. The door started bulging as if they were using the car to push it in.

CHAPTER 49: FOURTH OF JULY

"Ready?" Thor shouted. "Fire in the hole! Damn it, Elbow, that's *you*! Light it up!"

Elbow set the business end of the torch to the first orange wire. It fizzed like a sparkler, traveled up the wall and across the ceiling. Elbow was mesmerized watching it.

"For God's sake, man, take cover!" Thor yelled.

Elbow dived under the kitchen card table. The wall above the door suddenly exploded sending bricks and dirt hurling in outside. The door collapsed onto the car. To top it off, Andy let go of a large chain and the remains of the awning along with loose bricks came crashing down on top of the black car.

"Light the second one...*Now!*" Thor shouted.

Elbow crawled over to the orange wires with the torch. He hesitantly touched the torch to the second wire, hurriedly crawled back under the table and covered his head.

The second explosion set off a billowing mass of orange smoke that flowed out into the parking lot. It smelled like sulfur and made him cough. The guys outside under the awing and debris were coughing too.

Elbow dropped the welding torch and made a run for the stairs. He could see people running through the smoke. A shot rang out. It careened off one of the steel rafters and hit the brick wall next to his shoulder. Not being fond of explosions or bullets, he took the hint and disappeared into Red's upstairs studio, slamming the door behind him.

Red was still stretched out on the sofa, oblivious to the drama down on the warehouse floor. Best to leave him there. There was a hatch to the roof somewhere up on the second floor and this seemed like a good time to use it. Going out the door was not an option. Elbow scanned the studio ceiling. No hatch.

In the bedroom, Tiffany had slipped into a pair of tight leggings and a tee shirt. Elbow searched the bedroom ceiling. The rusted hatch was in the far corner.

"What's going on?" Tiffany wanted to know. "Was that a shot?"

"Some of the invaders got trigger happy, but the shot went wild. Help me pile up this chair on the table over there so I can open the roof hatch."

"The roof? Why the roof?"

"Because the bad guys are down there with guns and the roof is up here and I don't want to be down there," he explained while assembling the chair on the table. The logic was simple. He had an aversion to getting holes in his skin. The roof seemed a better bet than the door.

She helped steady the chair as he climbed up near the ceiling and pushed up on the rusty hatch. If there was a lock on it he was cooked. There wasn't, and he could finally feel it give way against the crust of debris around the sides. One more shove and it popped open showering a cascade of rust, leaves and water into the room. Sunlight and the humid smell of a bright Florida morning poured in. Elbow wasted no time getting himself into the opening and out on the roof.

"I don't want to stay here if people are downstairs with guns! Help me up too," Tiffany said. "Wait—I've got to get my purse."

Elbow sighed. "I've got to go!"

He was just about to shut the hatch when she climbed up on the chair and reached for his hand. Against his better judgement he grabbed her arm. She hung on as the chair she was standing on tipped and fell off the table. Elbow almost fell back in the hole but managed to pull her up through the opening until she could sit on the roof.

"God, It's filthy up here," she said.

"Help me close this thing."

She took the other side of the hatch and together they shoved it back into place.

"Oh damn, I broke a nail."

"More than that will get broken if they find us." Elbow gestured for her to be quiet as he carefully lay down and peered over the edge of the roof to survey the parking lot.

The large black car, covered in bricks, was still parked in front of the steel door. Orange smoke poured out. Four guys, Miguel among them, staggered through the orange fog trying to breathe.

Elbow backed up from the edge of the roof and thought for a moment. "Tiffany, can you climb down a pipe?" he whispered.

She smiled. "Honey, I used to be a pole dancer. What have you got in mind?"

He smiled and led her over to the back corner of the building. If he remembered correctly, there was a pipe there going all the way down to the ground he once snagged his jeans on. It was still there and felt solid. He checked that none of the muscled crew was stationed in the back. The coast was clear.

Elbow nodded for Tiffany to start over the edge of the roof. She was about to grab the pipe when the entire building vibrated with another explosion.

"What the hell was that?" Elbow yelled, then quickly grabbed Tiffany to keep her from going over the edge the hard way.

"Looks like Thor got a little too enthusiastic with the gunpowder," she said. "He makes great Fourth of July fireworks."

"Fireworks?"

Elbow crawled over to the front edge of the roof again to steal a look. The last explosion blew all the window glass out into the parking lot. The invaders were still dazed, rising up, staggering like dusty zombies.

CHAPTER 50: CIRCUS ACT

It was definitely time to go. Better hurry before the gunmen recovered, the neighborhood got curious or some do-gooder called the fire department. Elbow headed over to the escape pipe at the edge of the roof.

Tiffany blew him a kiss, threw her baggy purse over her shoulder, grabbed the pipe, and deftly lowered herself over the roof edge. She was an expert. He watched her descend and imagined what she looked like on stage. He wondered if she was ever a cat burglar too. When she reached the ground he motioned for her to stay close to the building.

Another explosion went off inside the warehouse, this time the building shuddered. Puffs of orange smoke and sparkly flashes of light spouted up through holes in the roof.

Elbow quickly lowered himself over the edge of the roof and clung to the pipe. His pole technique wasn't nearly as graceful as Tiffany's. He caught his shoe behind the pipe once and had to pull it free. The pipe suddenly let go, depositing Elbow ungracefully, butt-first, on the ground. At least he was down.

They made their way to the front and peeked around the corner where tall weeds concealed them. A fresh volume of orange smoke was pouring out all the doors and windows. Miguel's men were still trying to disentangle themselves from the pile of bricks and not too focused on anything but getting loose from the collapsed awning, but they were still between Elbow and Tiffany and the blue Mustang.

"Thor really did a number on the warehouse," Elbow whispered. "Who is he anyway?"

"Didn't Red tell you? Thor is former Special Ops. He has the whole place rigged. Thor's a bit of a nut about it. He was also nuts about Cici last night. She's safe. Those goons won't get any farther than the door."

"You mean we didn't have to go crawling out on the roof and down that pipe like a circus act?"

She grinned. "If we're going, now would be a good time. Those guys will be busy for a while."

Elbow looked up. "Damn! Thor and Cici and Andy are crawling out a shattered window at the other end of the warehouse. We've got to do something to distract the gunmen!"

Tiffany opened her purse.

"Now isn't a good time to go looking for lipstick," Elbow complained.

She smiled. "This is something better." She took out several, small, round balls, like golf balls. "Thor gave me these," she said. She stood up and threw one in a tall looping arc that landed smack on top of the black car. It exploded like a flash cap, splattering blue smoke and paint over Miguel's posse.

Elbow gave her a kiss. "Nice throw. Can I try one of those?"

"Sure." She gave him another ball.

Elbow stood up and whistled. One of the gunmen turned around and WHAM, Elbow zinged one square in the middle of the guy's forehead. The guy was stunned, temporarily blinded and fell back into the pile. It was just enough to let the warehouse inhabitants skirt unnoticed along the other side of the building toward the blue mustang.

Suddenly a barrage of little paint balls from their direction rained down on the hapless gunmen, exploding in a steaming mass of blue, orange and green smoke and paint. Thor and Andy were good shots. The gunmen who had worked themselves free were busy wiping paint out of their eyes and off their pretty black suits.

Elbow grabbed Tiffany's hand. Keeping low, they made a run for it behind the black car toward the blue Mustang. Thor, Andy, and Cici headed for the blue car too and dove in the back seat while Elbow and Tiffany jumped in front.

"Damn! The car keys are in the warehouse!" Elbow yelled.

Tiffany smiled. "Looks like somebody bypassed the ignition already." A panel of plastic was missing from the steering column and loose wires hung underneath.

Elbow fiddled with the wires trying to fit them together.

Tiffany reached for the wires. "Here, try these two," she said.

The car roared to life.

How lucky could a guy get. Tiffany was a woman of amazing talents after his own heart. She could climb poles, make a guy's head swim in bed, jack start a car and carried exploding paint balls in her purse. What other talents did she have? He put the car in gear and backed up.

A thunderous explosion shook the ground. The warehouse roof split open. Multicolored fireworks spewed into the sky. Without the roof, the outside walls of the warehouse started collapsing outward, like dominoes in slow motion. First the back wall, then the sidewalls and finally the front wall collapsed. Like a final cosmic hammer, the last of the wall of bricks above the door fell on top of the black car. The only thing left standing was Red's second story apartment block in the middle.

Everyone in the car sat starring at the carnage. They were speechless.

"It blow up," Cici said, breaking the silence.

"Where did you leave the welding torch, Elbow?" Thor asked.

The welding torch. Where did he leave it? Elbow thought for a moment. He just tossed it aside when he made a quick exit up the stairs to get on the roof. Maybe it was in the direction of the orange wires, maybe near the plastic sheets around his room or... Better not dwell on that point.

Sirens whined in the distance.

Above the billowing smoke, the door to Red's apartment flew open. Red stood in the doorway at the top of the stairs surveying the smoldering rubble and blue sky above him. Elbow raised his hand and gave Red a little wave. Red waved back and started down the stairs which were somehow still standing. He stumbled across the bricks and over the black car toward the Mustang.

Red looked dazed as he leaned up against the car. "Was there an earthquake?" He squeaked.

"We'll tell you all about it," Tiffany said as she opened the car door and pulled him into the front seat.

The blue Mustang now had more people in it than a clown car. It hung a little low with all the people squeezed inside, but as long as the tires held up they were good. Elbow put the car in drive and pealed out of the parking lot into the alley and then to the main street.

"So... Where to?" Elbow asked.

"You ever been to Disney World?" Tiffany asked. "I hear it's just like paradise. I always wanted to be Snow White."

"Snow White was never a pole dancer."

"Who says?" She winked.

Elbow smiled. In the rear view mirror, he could see flashing lights. Fire trucks, squad cars and ambulances were screaming their way to the warehouse. Best not to be anywhere near there when they arrived.

He headed for the highway north. They were on their way to paradise. What could go wrong?

THE END